# Age of extInction

By
Mark Gomes

Copyright © 2025 Mark Gomes

All rights reserved. No part of this book may be reproduced.

ISBN-13:978-1-0684158-0-7

# TABLE OF CONTENTS

"The saddest aspect of life right now is that science gathers knowledge faster than society gathers wisdom."

— Isaac Asimov

Disclaimer:

This work is a fictional exploration of the societal and economic impacts of artificial intelligence. While many technological trends and projections are based on real-world research and analysis, some outcomes have been dramatized for narrative effect. The author has grounded speculative elements in credible sources, but specific future projections should be viewed as creative interpretations rather than definitive predictions.

# PROLOGUE

**Extinction-Level Event.**

It is a term that carries weight, though most never truly consider its meaning. It refers to a moment in time—a disruption so vast that it erases life as it was, replacing it with something else, or nothing at all. A scar in history that divides before and after. These events are not always sudden, nor are they always understood in their time. Some unfold violently, others quietly, but their impact is always the same. Life changes. Forever.

The Earth's past is littered with such moments. The Great Oxygenation Event, 2.5 billion years ago, when cyanobacteria flooded the planet's atmosphere with oxygen, wiping out species unable to adapt. The Permian Extinction, 252 million years ago, when volcanic activity released greenhouse gases so toxic that 90% of marine life and 70% of terrestrial species were lost. The Ice Ages, cycles of frost and famine that reshaped continents and populations. But the most famous extinction-level event—the one etched into humanity's collective imagination—is the one that ended the age of the dinosaurs.

66 million years ago, an asteroid fell from the sky.

It struck near what we now call the Yucatán Peninsula, unleashing devastation at a scale our modern minds can barely comprehend. The asteroid's impact marked the trigger event, a single moment that would cascade into the end of 75% of life on Earth.

From that point, the stages of extinction followed with brutal inevitability:

Impact: A blinding flash, the force of billions of nuclear bombs released in an instant.

Dust Clouds: Smoke, ash, and debris surged into the atmosphere, blocking the sun and plunging the Earth into darkness. Plants

withered, unable to photosynthesize.
Volcanic Eruptions: The impact set off tectonic chaos—volcanoes spewed molten rock and toxic gases, compounding the damage.
Mass Extinction: Food chains collapsed. The strong starved alongside the weak. The world grew still, its skies empty of flight and its forests silent.
The Great Dying: When the dust finally settled, the Earth was unrecognizable, its ecosystems shattered. Only fragments of life endured—small, resilient creatures that would become the architects of what came next.
What the dinosaurs experienced then was not unique. It was simply their turn. Every species, every civilization, eventually faces its own extinction-level event. For some, it comes from the outside: an asteroid, a flood, a fire. For others, it comes from within.
And now it is humanity's turn.
This time, there is no asteroid. No smoking crater to mark the moment history shifted.
This extinction did not arrive from the sky. It came as a whisper in the wires.
And it began not with an asteroid, but with a line of code.
The impact has already happened. The dust clouds are rising. The structures of civilization are shifting beneath our feet.
This is the Age of Extinction

***"Extinction is the rule. Survival is the exception."***
***— Carl Sagan***

# STAGE 1: TRIGGER EVENT – AI'S SUDDEN INTRODUCTION

## Stage 1: Trigger Event – AI's Sudden Introduction (macro view)

Humanity's asteroid wasn't a celestial object—it was a technological rupture.
The arrival of advanced artificial intelligence didn't come as a gradual evolution—it was a singularity. AI systems capable of independent thought, creativity, and optimization beyond human speed arrived not merely as tools, but as catalysts—an extinction-level event cloaked in the guise of progress.

For a brief moment, AI was celebrated.
It promised progress.
It promised abundance.
But like the asteroid, AI wasn't just a tool—it was a trigger.

**The Year That Changed Everything**
2024 marked the inflection point. AI models surpassed one trillion parameters, achieving capabilities that rivaled human cognitive functions in creative and analytical tasks.

Huawei's PanGu-Σ, at 1.085 trillion parameters, demonstrated creative problem-solving and language generation beyond human speed. OpenAI's GPT-4.5 and Google DeepMind's Gemini followed, competing in cognitive complexity and processing speed. (Wikipedia, 2024)

AI adoption accelerated faster than any previous technological shift.
Harvard Business Review reported that AI adoption across business functions grew from 50% to 56% within 18 months—

exceeding the pace of previous industrial revolutions. (HBR, 2021)

The speed was staggering—and devastating.

AI-driven companies in Silicon Valley surpassed a combined $1.5 trillion in market value by the end of 2024—outpacing the dot-com bubble. Nvidia's market cap alone soared from $1.2 trillion at the end of 2023 to $3.28 trillion by the end of 2024, driven by AI infrastructure demand. OpenAI, Anthropic, and other AI-focused startups collectively raised over $100 billion within 18 months. (Reuters, 2024)

According to McKinsey, AI integration increased corporate productivity by 22% in just two years. But at a human cost—workforce reductions averaged 35% in industries adopting AI automation. (McKinsey, 2024)

**The First Shockwaves**

AI efficiency came at a brutal human cost.

- Content Creation: AI-driven platforms like Adobe Firefly and OpenAI's DALL-E replaced 40% of graphic designers, copywriters, and editors within 18 months. Adobe reported a 40% reduction in human creative roles by mid-2025. (TechCrunch, 2025)
- Customer Service: AI chatbots eliminated 30% of call center roles within a year. By mid-2025, over 1.2 million customer service jobs in the U.S. had been automated. (McKinsey, 2025)
- Software Development: AI-assisted coding tools cut junior developer demand by 50% in under two years. GitHub Copilot and OpenAI Codex automated over 40% of standard coding tasks. (TechCrunch, 2025)

"AI adoption is accelerating faster than labor markets can adapt," Brookings warned in 2024. (Brookings, 2024)

**Economic Output – The Artificial Boom**

The financial upside was undeniable—for those positioned to benefit.

AI-integrated companies saw productivity soar by 22%. But workforce reductions created a net loss in human labor. In sectors dominated by automation, the benefits flowed upward—toward corporations and shareholders—while the displaced workforce was left behind.

In Silicon Valley alone, AI-driven startups amassed a combined valuation exceeding $1.5 trillion in just 36 months—outpacing the growth of the dot-com era. Nvidia alone added over $2 trillion in market value between 2023 and 2024. (Reuters, 2024)

"Industry analysts suggest that the winners in AI adoption are those with specialized skills. For everyone else, displacement is inevitable." (The Economist, 2025)

**The Job Displacement Cascade**

Lower-tier jobs evaporated first.

- 5 million jobs were eliminated globally within two years of AI's mainstream adoption, according to World Economic Forum projections. (WEF, 2024)
- Mid-tier jobs: Projected losses to reach 8 million as AI encroached on managerial and cognitive roles. (WEF, 2024)
- AI Skill Divide: Demand for AI-focused roles—such as machine learning engineers and data scientists—rose 600%. (The Economist, 2025)
- Only 2% of displaced workers had the qualifications to transition. (McKinsey, 2025)

"AI-driven job displacement is following a predictable pattern," McKinsey noted. "Automation is climbing the value chain, from repetitive tasks to decision-making roles." (McKinsey, 2025)

**The Social Fallout**

Public trust in AI collapsed as reports of AI hallucinations, biased decisions, and systemic failures mounted.
Yet 68% of businesses refused to roll back AI reliance, citing cost efficiency as paramount.

The social cost escalated rapidly.
Mass protests erupted in 37 countries as entire industries vanished in real time.

In the American Midwest, AI adoption in manufacturing hubs caused regional economic strain, driving unemployment toward levels not seen since the Great Depression. (MIT Sloan, 2024)

"Governments are not moving fast enough to regulate AI," The Guardian warned. "Corporate AI integration outpaces public policy by a dangerous margin." (The Guardian, 2024)

**The Final Statistic**

By 2025, AI adoption outpaced policy regulation by an estimated factor of 100:1—rendering governments reactive rather than proactive. (Brookings, UK Parliament Report, 2025)

### *Stage 1: Trigger Event - AI's Sudden Introduction (micro view)*

*The soft hum of her laptop filled the quiet apartment as Sophia Lee sat at her kitchen table, fingers hovering over the keyboard. Outside, Harmony Falls was alive with the sounds of another ordinary day--children laughing, a dog barking, distant traffic. Inside, everything was still.*

*Her coffee sat untouched, a ring of dried foam staining the rim. The email on her screen was blunt, clinical.*

*Dear Contractors,*

*We're excited to announce that we're integrating generative AI into our design process. This cutting-edge tool will streamline our workflow, allowing us to deliver faster, more cost-effective solutions to our clients. Unfortunately, this means we'll be reducing our need for external designers. We thank you for your contributions and wish you all the best in your future endeavors.*

*She read it again, but the words didn't change. Generative AI. Reducing our need. Thank you for your contributions.*

*It was over.*

*Her eyes flicked to the shelf across the room, to a framed photo from her first gallery opening. She had been smiling, holding up an abstract painting, surrounded by friends. That was eight years ago, back when she believed art would define her life. Then came reality--bills, student loans, the need for something stable. Freelance graphic design wasn't her dream, but it had been hers. It had been enough. Now, even that was gone.*

*Her fingers drifted to the laptop, where a cursor blinked in an empty search bar. She typed "AI graphic design platforms" and hit enter. The first result boasted "Professional-quality logos in seconds for only $9.99!" Nine ninety-nine. She had charged $400 for her last logo.*

*Clicking the link, she watched the interface guide her through the process. It was sleek, efficient, effortless. In minutes, the AI had created a clean, modern design. She wanted to hate it. But the truth pressed against her chest, cold and certain. It was better than her. Faster than her. And it would never stop.*

*Her phone buzzed. "Hey, sweetheart," her mother's voice was warm, familiar. "Just checking in. How's work?"*

*Sophia swallowed hard. "Fine," she lied.*

*"Good, good," her mom said. "You know, I saw one of your logos on that café downtown. It looks amazing. Your dad and I are so proud of you."*

*Sophia forced a smile she knew her mother couldn't see. "Thanks, Mom." They chatted for a few more minutes before hanging up. As the call ended, Sophia stared at her hands--hands that had once held brushes, sketched designs, built something from nothing. Hands that felt suddenly useless. For the first time in years, she thought about her old art supplies--dusty tubes of acrylics, forgotten canvases stacked in her closet. Maybe she could paint again. Not to sell. Just to feel something. But even as the thought formed, she shook it away. She couldn't afford indulgences like that anymore.*

*Across the street, the Scent Technologies innovation center glowed, its glass doors sliding open and shut as workers streamed in and out. There was movement, efficiency, purpose. She wondered what it felt like to be part of something like that.*

*Her laptop chimed with another notification. A new gig posting. 100 social media graphics. 48-hour turnaround. $5 per graphic. Sophia stared at the screen. Five dollars. It was insulting. Degrading. She clicked "apply" anyway.*

*The asteroid had struck. The shockwaves were only just beginning.*

*For Sophia, it wasn't just the loss of work. It was the death of something she hadn't realized she was clinging to--the belief that her creativity, her skills, her humanity still had value. The asteroid that wiped out the dinosaurs hadn't ended everything in an instant. It set off a chain reaction--a slow unraveling that no one could stop.*

# CHAPTER 1

***We** are human-lobsters in an AI techno-soup naively thinking it will nourish our future as it slowly boils us into irrelevance.*

Professor Robert Jansen wondered if having a lobster tank on stage would reinforce his opening remark. He shrugged it off, nothing short of an alien life form could help. No one was here to see him, it was the tech bro rockstar Nolan Scent, his keynote co-speaker. He was using Power Point. Scent would probably have an AI generated virtual reality space that would have everyone so agog with amazement that all the speeches would be redundant. Redundant. A big part of why Jansen was here. He took a deep breath to halt his self-inflicted intimidation. Then in a room with no windows and a closed door he felt the faintest of breezes ever so briefly on his face and he knew he was where he needed to be.

Victim: Homo Sapiens
Cause of Death: Suicide
Date of Death: Ongoing

The stark words hung on the massive screen, casting a long shadow over the 8,000-strong audience gathered in Stanford University's Frost Amphitheater. Excited murmurs gave way to silence, faces tense, breaths stilled. Jansen standing at the podium, let the quiet linger, scanning the crowd. "Weapon," he said at last, his voice calm but sharp enough to cut through the hush. He paused, letting the word land before adding, "Artificial intelligence." A ripple of groans and scattered laughter followed. He raised a hand, not to silence them, but as if to acknowledge their resistance. "Not in the way you think. No more than the dinosaurs--who roamed this earth as the dominant species for 135 million years--would have seen an asteroid as their weapon of mass extinction."

The screen behind him shifted to an image of a massive asteroid impact, fires blazing, skies choked with ash. Jansen clicked a remote, and a number appeared in bold: 0.0000116. "That's Manhattan's surface area as a percentage of the Earth's. Eleven-millionths of one percent. The same as that of the asteroid that wiped out the dinosaurs. A fraction so small it's barely comprehensible. Yet it was enough. Enough to unleash a chain of events that destroyed nearly every dinosaur on the planet. Not immediately. Not everywhere. Most of them never saw, heard, or even felt the asteroid strike. But its consequences became inescapable." He paused again, letting the image of the impact linger before clicking the remote once more. A timeline appeared, stark and simple: Trigger Event → Immediate Effects → Ecosystem Disruption → Long-Term Change.

"This is the lifecycle of an extinction-level event. An ELE. It starts with a trigger event. A small disruption--a strike, a fissure, a spark--that sets off something far larger. The dinosaurs couldn't stop what followed. But we..." His voice softened, drawing the audience in. "We have introduced our own trigger event. Artificial Intelligence. And unlike them, we know it's happening. The question is whether we act." The silence was taut, broken only by the faint hum of whispers. A few scattered boos followed, a lone voice shouting, "Propaganda!" Jansen smiled faintly, unfazed.

"Dinosaurs had their asteroid. We have ours. But it isn't falling from the sky--it's rising from within. And if you think this is hyperbole, consider this: the Age of AI will not arrive with a bang. It's already here, already reshaping our environment, our economies, our minds. And yet we, like the dinosaurs before us, fail to grasp its full impact." He clicked again, the screen shifting to images of ash-covered landscapes, barren forests, and the ghostly outlines of fossilized skeletons. "The difference is choice. Dinosaurs had none. We do. The question isn't whether AI will change the world--it's why we're allowing it to. Why are we so eager to cede control of our own narrative?"

He paused, his next words quiet but deliberate. "Why do we build? Why do we create? Why, in the face of a collapsing future, do we still... have children?" The audience stirred uneasily, some leaning forward, others crossing their arms. But before Jansen could press further, a rustle from the far end of the stage drew his attention. He stopped mid-thought, the words stolen from his lips. The screen went dark. The audience began to stir as all eyes turned to a figure emerging from the wings, stepping into the light with the assuredness of someone who owned the room--and maybe the future.

Nolan Scent

The applause came swiftly, loud and thunderous, a standing ovation that swept through the amphitheater like wildfire. Jansen remained at the podium, his face unreadable, as Nolan strode onto the stage, smiling faintly. Jansen stepped back, his moment eclipsed, as Nolan reached for the microphone. The billionaire surveyed the crowd, letting the energy swell. When he spoke, his voice was warm, effortless, and unyielding.

"Let's talk about what's next," Nolan said. And with that, the spotlight shifted.

#

Nolan Scent had watched Jansen from the wings. Jansen was dangerous. This crowd were not a measure for Jansen's message. These bright young things who believed the future owed each of them a fortune, were not people who would genuinely consider the idea of an AI-driven future having parallels to an extinction level event. Nolan always thought Jansen's pitch was too grand and too abstract. Dinosaurs were as real as aliens for most people, they existed in movies and books. In the case of dinosaurs, museums too, but who went to museums nowadays. Jansen's message in the towns where jobs were being lost to AI driven automation and efficiency, they would drink his Koolaid all day long. *Why do we still have children?*

That was new. That had to be crushed.

Dressed in a tailored navy suit, his presence exuded the polished confidence of a man who had reshaped the world in his image. As the founder and CEO of Scent Technologies, the globe's largest AI enterprise, he was a symbol of relentless ambition and success.

The Scent family name had been prominent in business circles for generations, but Nolan had elevated it beyond its old-money roots. While his family's wealth came from traditional industries, Nolan's brilliance had turned him into the architect of the AI age. Under his leadership, Scent Technologies had revolutionized sectors from healthcare to manufacturing, creating a vast empire that spanned continents.

Yet, behind his composed exterior was a man marked by personal tragedy. Two decades earlier, his wife Rebecca had died giving birth to their only child, Molly. Her death had been a cruel twist to what should have been the most joyous moment of his life. In the years since, Nolan had rarely spoken of her, burying his grief beneath layers of steel ambition. Molly, now an adult, was his only family, though their relationship often bore the strain of his towering expectations.

#

Jansen slipped out of the amphitheater before the applause had fully faded. The manicured pathways of Stanford offered no comfort, their neatness a sharp contrast to the disarray in his mind. Nolan had the crowd now, the spotlight, the stage. That was how it always went. He didn't belong in those moments, not really.

The late afternoon sun cast long shadows across the lawns as he made his way back to his office. Students cycled past, conversations and laughter floating on the breeze. He walked with his hands in his pockets, his gaze fixed just ahead, moving with the kind of purpose that didn't invite interruptions. Jansen had always been a tall man, but there was something about the way he moved--something unassuming, as if he were trying to take up less space than he had. It wasn't a conscious thing, just the way life leaves its marks on some people, pressing them inward. He reached the familiar doorway of the archaeology department and stepped inside, letting the door click shut behind him. For a moment, he stood there, staring at the cluttered bulletin board across the hall. Meetings. Lectures. Notices. Life going on. Then he turned toward his office, the same path he'd taken every day, his thoughts already slipping into the past.

Five years ago, on the morning of his 35th birthday, Robert had stood tall. He had woken at his dig site on the Hell Creek Formation in Montana, feeling like the happiest man alive. Beneath his feet lay a fossil bed that promised wonders--a discovery sparked by an underground fissure opened during aggressive mining operations by Scent Technologies. Early imaging hinted at something extraordinary, perhaps even the holy grail of paleontology: a Tyrannosaurus rex.

For Robert, this was a once-in-a-lifetime opportunity, a chance to help rewrite history. The find had drawn national attention, thrusting him into a spotlight he hadn't sought but secretly relished. That morning, as he guided his wife and two young daughters around the site, explaining the marvels that might lie beneath the surface, he'd felt something he rarely allowed himself: joy.

The site buzzed with activity, the clatter of tools and the low murmur of voices mixing with the dry Montana air. There had been concerns, of course--questions about the stability of the ground, murmurs about the risks of digging too close to the fissure. But caution often clashed with the urgency of discovery, and the team had pressed on. He never saw it coming. The ground beneath them shifted, suddenly and violently, as if the earth itself had exhaled. A crack widened with terrifying speed, the fractured landscape giving way. His last clear memory was reaching for his daughters, their laughter still ringing in his ears, the world tilting as the ground fell away.

When Robert awoke, he was at the bottom of the sinkhole. The air was thick with dust, and his body was heavy with pain. His mind, though, was strangely clear, replaying what he thought he'd seen--his family, their faces vivid in his memory, frozen mid-reach, mid-laugh, mid-life. He wanted to call out to them, but his voice felt trapped in his chest. Then, faintly, he felt it. A breeze, impossibly soft, brushing against his face. It was the barest whisper of air, cutting through the stillness, and for a moment he thought he saw movement--something shifting, fading, leaving. The sensation stirred something deep inside him, though he could not name it then. He closed his eyes, too weak to fight the pull of unconsciousness, and let the wind carry him into darkness. When he was pulled from the sinkhole hours later, he was alive, but the man he had been was gone. The earth had taken everything, and in its place, it had left him with silence--and the faint memory of that fleeting breeze.

Now, five years later, he had become a voice for those who saw the cracks forming beneath humanity's feet. Just as the asteroid had been an extinction-level event for the dinosaurs, he believed artificial intelligence could trigger one for humanity--not with a single impact, but with a cascade of disruptions that would collapse the systems holding society together. And like the sinkhole that had swallowed his family, it would begin without warning. Like lobsters, never realizing the beginning of the end is upon them because the water feels so lovely and warm.

#

Nolan Scent stepped to the podium with a quiet confidence that drew the audience's attention before he spoke a word. He paused, letting the weight of Professor Jansen's words linger in the amphitheater. The anticipation in the crowd was palpable, a tension he would shape into something far more useful. Finally, his smile broke--a small, deliberate gesture--and he began.

"Thank you, Professor Jansen, for your thoughtful exploration of where we stand as a species," Nolan said, his voice measured, steady. "It's clear we're at a crossroads, a pivotal moment in human history. And yes," he added with a nod, "the professor is right--we are facing an extinction-level event."

The murmurs of the crowd swelled, a mix of apprehension and curiosity. Nolan's gaze swept across the audience, not rushing to explain.

"But," he said, his tone shifting slightly, drawing them in, "where some see catastrophe, I see possibility. Where some fear the end, I see the beginning of something profoundly greater."

Behind him, the screen lit up, showing scenes of a vibrant, bustling metropolis. The crowd's murmurs stilled. The cityscape faded into the interior of a smart hospital: doctors working seamlessly with AI-driven systems, a man walking confidently with the help of neural implants. Nolan turned, gesturing toward the images.

"Imagine a world where healthcare is no longer reactive but predictive. Where illness is caught before it strikes, and suffering--the kind that has plagued humanity for millennia--becomes a rarity."

He turned back to the audience, his voice softening as he let the images speak. "This isn't the stuff of science fiction. It's happening now." The screen shifted to sprawling farmland, drones zipping across fields as they monitored crops and distributed resources with precision. The efficiency was dazzling: no waste, no famine, only abundance. "Take agriculture," Nolan said, the quiet passion in his tone building. "With AI, we can meet one of humanity's oldest challenges: feeding the world. Not just enough to survive, but enough to thrive."

The audience leaned forward, captivated by the vision unfolding before them. Nolan clicked the remote again, and the screen filled with a simulation: a Chicxulub-like asteroid streaking toward Earth. "Now," he said, his voice deepening, "imagine another kind of challenge. An asteroid, hurtling toward us--a disaster on the scale that ended the reign of the dinosaurs. Would we be ready? Could we act in time?" He let the question hang in the air before answering it himself. "A future empowered by AI would give us a fighting chance. Not just to survive, but to prevail."

The screen changed again, this time to a city of the future: traffic moving seamlessly, energy flowing cleanly, justice systems operating efficiently under AI governance. It was a vision of utopia--or, at the very least, something close to it. "This," Nolan said, pacing slowly across the stage, "is what AI offers us: a world where inefficiency, waste, and inequality are relics of the past. A world not ruled by machines, but guided by human ingenuity, enhanced by the tools we've created."

He paused, turning to face the audience directly. "AI isn't an invader. It's a mirror of our best selves. It's the embodiment of our curiosity, our drive, our ingenuity. And yes, there are risks--but as Darwin taught us, survival belongs to those who adapt. This isn't about fear. It's about mastery." His final words were quieter, but no less resonant. "This is about survival--not just of the strongest, but of the smartest. Of those who can see the horizon and seize the opportunity."

The applause began tentatively, then grew into a thunderous ovation. The crowd was transfixed, not just by Nolan's words but by the world he had conjured--a future so close they could almost touch it. Nolan smiled, his expression calm and assured, as if to say, of course you believe. *You're smart enough to see it.*

##

# CHAPTER 2

The hum of the Bentley's engine was barely audible as Molly Scent leaned back against the quilted leather seats; her gaze fixed on the tablet balanced on her lap. The news anchor's voice echoed through the car's surround speakers, crisp and clinical.

"In Harmony Falls, minor protests broke out today as local businesses struggled to compete with Scent Technologies' AI-driven operations," the anchor reported. Onscreen, grainy footage showed a handful of workers holding signs outside a family-run machining shop. The slogans were predictable: Humans Over Machines, Jobs Not Bots. The camera panned to a middle-aged woman in a diner apron speaking into a microphone, her voice trembling with frustration.

Molly muted the audio and glanced at her driver, who maintained a steady focus on the road. She closed the tablet with a flick of her manicured fingers, her thoughts turning to the town.

Harmony Falls, she mused. A textbook example of her father's vision at work: businesses optimized by AI integration, neural chips enhancing productivity and satisfaction, and the inevitable march of automation reshaping the landscape. The protests were predictable, but inconsequential. Growing pains, her father called them. She had come to see them as an almost necessary phase--resistance always preceded progress.

The Bentley approached the towering glass facade of Scent Technologies Global HQ, a shimmering monolith of steel and innovation, dominating the skyline. The vast entrance plaza was a study in efficiency--autonomous security drones hovered silently above the gates, biometric scanners processed employees without pause, and the company's insignia, an abstracted infinity loop, glowed blue against the dark glass.

Molly tucked her tablet into her bag. Welcome to the future.

#

The conference room was already filled with senior executives by the time Nolan Scent strode to the head of the table. The air carried the sterile hum of efficiency--data streams flickering across embedded displays, silent notifications syncing across neural interfaces.

"Should we begin?" Dr. Victor Han asked, glancing at the empty chair beside Nolan.

Nolan's fingers tapped against the polished surface. "Yes."

Then the door opened.

Molly walked in, unhurried, the confidence of someone who belonged yet hadn't rushed to prove it. Nolan looked up instinctively, and for a fraction of a second--a second too long--he saw her as something else.

The way she moved. Her posture, the way she carried herself, the unconscious tilt of her head as she scanned the room. It was Rebecca, years ago, standing by a fish stand, laughing, radiant in the Mediterranean sun.

The memory came so fast, so sharp, Nolan almost let it take him. Almost.

He shut it down.

"Apologies," Molly said, sliding into the seat beside him, her voice light. "You know how private jets are. Such a hassle."

The tension snapped. A few executives chuckled. Nolan exhaled, nodding curtly. "Try commercial next time. Builds character."

She flashed him a knowing look before turning her attention to the meeting, seamlessly taking her place.

#

Lucas Bennett, Head of Infrastructure, cleared his throat. "To bring you up to speed, we're at 48% AI-integrated workforce adoption in Harmony Falls businesses, all directly or indirectly under Scent Technologies."

"Resistance?" Nolan asked.

Dr. Viktor Han adjusted his neural visor. "It's growing. Not enough to destabilize the initiative, but there's still hesitation among the remaining workforces. Some holdouts claim human oversight is 'necessary' in certain fields."

Molly crossed her legs, resting her hands on the table. "Necessary? Or just preferred?"

Han gave her a measured nod. "Preferred, for now. But preference erodes with exposure. Once AI optimization becomes standard, human involvement becomes an anomaly, not an expectation."

Nolan steepled his fingers. "And the chips?"

"The opt-in rates are still under projection, but we expect Harmony Falls to hit 65% adoption by Q3. Early reports indicate increased efficiency, reduced resistance, and--" Han paused. "--more consistent behavioral alignment."

Molly arched a brow. "Meaning?"

Lucas fielded that one. "We're seeing a drop in workplace conflict, fewer resignations, and higher compliance. Chip-enhanced employees display a measurable decrease in stress factors related to AI adoption. In short, they adjust faster."

Dr. Neha Patel, Head of AI Cultural Systems, took over next. "Entertainment adoption is following projections. The majority of content engagement in Harmony Falls is now AI-generated. Predictive feedback loops are fully operational. Active consumption is decreasing. Passive engagement is rising."

Nobody forced people to watch AI-generated content. It was just easier. Easier than thinking. Easier than deciding. Easier than pushing back. No one needed to control public sentiment. It was already adapting.

Nolan had remained silent throughout the reports. When he finally spoke, his voice was calm, deliberate. "We are not changing the world. We are correcting its inefficiencies."

A pause.

"People fear change. But they fear uncertainty more. Stability is the greatest currency. We don't need to force compliance. We need to remove the conditions that allow resistance to exist."

Molly felt the certainty in his words settle over the room.

A beat of silence. The weight of what was being said was not lost on anyone.

"Good," Nolan said finally, his voice unreadable.

##

The mansion was quiet as Molly entered through the side entrance, her heels clicking softly against the marble floor. It was a deliberate quiet, curated by the house staff to maintain the illusion of serenity amidst the chaos outside. She made her way to the study, the only room in the house where her father allowed clutter--papers, books, and files stacked on every available surface. It was his controlled chaos, a reflection of his mind.

Nolan Scent stood by the window, backlit by the fading evening light. He turned as she entered, his expression unreadable but his presence commanding as always. "How was the trip?" he asked without preamble, his voice even. "Productive," Molly replied, setting her bag on the chair. "The new facilities in Asia are fully operational. Chip production is scaling faster than we projected. We'll meet the next quarter's targets, easily." Nolan nodded, pleased. "Good. That's critical. The demand will only grow once we roll out the next phase."

Molly crossed her arms, leaning against the desk. "Speaking of demand, how's the controlled experiment going? Harmony Falls seems to be making headlines."

"You heard Lucas's update, it's going as expected," Nolan said, turning back to the window. "It needs to get worse before it can be fixed." She raised an eyebrow. "Worse?" He turned to face her fully, his expression sharp. "People need to feel the chaos, Molly. They need to believe there's no alternative. Only then will they accept the solution."

"The solution being us, of course," she said dryly.

"Of course," Nolan replied, a faint smirk tugging at the corner of his mouth. "Speaking of chaos, did you see the speeches?" Molly's posture stiffened slightly. "I saw the highlights."

"And Jansen?" Nolan asked, his tone casual but his eyes keen. "What did you think of him?" "He's...passionate," Molly said carefully. "He knows how to connect with people. That makes him dangerous."

"Exactly," Nolan said, his voice low. He stepped closer, resting a hand on the edge of the desk. "I need you to get closer to him." She tilted her head, studying him. "Why?" Nolan's gaze didn't waver. "I don't want him increasing the volume before we have the fix in place with the President."

Molly frowned slightly, considering. "What kind of volume?" He didn't answer immediately, instead walking to a small safe behind his desk. He opened it with a quick series of taps and pulled out a thin folder, holding it out to her. "Did you hear his question?" Molly took the file but didn't open it immediately. She narrowed her eyes slightly. "Which question?" Nolan's silence was deliberate, his expression calculating. He wanted to see if she understood the stakes. Without missing a beat, she replied, "The one about what's the point of having children?" Nolan's lips curved into a faint smile. "Exactly. I don't want that gaining traction. If people start questioning their purpose, their legacy, it'll destabilize everything. Get him on-board with the benefits. If you can turn him, he'll be a powerful advocate."

Molly finally opened the folder, flipping through its pages. "Hard copy?" she asked with a smirk. "You could've emailed this."

"It's more secure than any electronic document," Nolan replied, his tone dismissive. She laughed softly, shaking her head. "Carrier pigeons next?"

"If that's what it takes. Tomorrow, I want you to get up to speed on Project Heal, especially the work of Professor Ethan Numan. Game-changer is an overused term but for his project it's not a big enough description. And when you're going through Jansen's file look into his near-death experience, it could be the angle you need."

Molly closed the file and met his gaze. "I'll handle it," she said, her tone steady. But as she left the study, the weight of the folder in her hand felt heavier than she expected. Jansen's question lingered in her mind, an echo she couldn't quite shake.

###

Harmony Falls was a town on the brink, a perfect microcosm of the challenges reshaping America. Nestled in the Midwest, it had once been a thriving industrial hub, its factories producing everything from precision tools to household goods. But those days were gone. Automation and AI had swept through the economy like a gale, displacing workers and gutting industries. Harmony Falls wasn't unique in its struggle; it was emblematic of a nation in crisis. And it was exactly the kind of place Nolan Scent needed.

Across Harmony Falls, independent businesses were floundering. Companies like Harmony Freight, a family-owned logistics firm, were caught in a perfect storm. Margins were tightening, customers demanding faster and cheaper services that only AI-automated competitors could deliver. Layoffs were common, morale was low, and worker solidarity began to crack under the weight of despair.

#

In the lunchroom at Harmony Freight, employees talked in hushed voices about rumors of a mass layoff. Jim Whelan, a truck dispatcher with two decades of experience, found himself unable to reassure his team. The pressures of maintaining human-driven schedules in an AI-dominated market were overwhelming. "We're dinosaurs," someone muttered. Jim didn't have the heart to disagree.

The strain rippled through the community. Moira Manley's diner saw fewer customers each week, her once-bustling establishment reduced to serving coffee to the same three regulars each morning. Families in Harmony Falls began selling homes that had been in the family for generations, chasing jobs that seemed further and further out of reach.

On paper, Nolan-owned businesses like Delta Precision Manufacturing and Harmony Care Solutions looked like beacons of stability. Metrics showed improved production times, reduced error rates, and efficiency gains compared to local competitors. Delta's factory lines hummed with activity, and the clinics at Harmony Care provided state-of-the-art diagnostics and treatments.

But even in these bastions of progress, cracks were forming. Workers at Delta Precision grumbled about looming automation, the company's AI-driven optimization plans casting a long shadow over their futures. Weekly workshops held by management explained upcoming changes, offering reassurances of "re-skilling opportunities" for displaced workers. These reassurances were met with equal parts skepticism and anger.

"Re-skilling?" one worker scoffed after a recent meeting. "They're just dressing it up to sound nice. What they mean is they've got nothing for us."

Despite the tension, the metrics still looked good. Employees at Delta continued to show up, morale hanging by a thread of hope and fear. Rachel Gardner, a young mother working the line, kept telling herself that things would work out. "At least we're still working," she told her husband, Tom. "That's more than most people can say."

What no one in Harmony Falls realized--not the workers, not the managers--was that the neural chips many of Scent Technology employees had voluntarily adopted weren't yet doing what they were designed to do. The chips had been sold as tools for enhancing workplace adaptability, reducing stress, and improving focus. And for now, that's all they were.

But Nolan Scent wasn't interested in temporary gains. Harmony Falls wasn't just an economic experiment--it was a controlled crisis. The chips' full capabilities, their ability to subtly recalibrate expectations and suppress dissatisfaction, remained dormant. Nolan was waiting. The labor unrest and community fractures weren't an obstacle to his plan--they were essential to it.

The crisis had to reach its peak. The town needed to feel the full weight of the disruption, the chaos of a society at the breaking point. Only then could Nolan step in with his solution--a solution that would appear like salvation but carry with it a price no one yet understood.

#

Lucas Bennett prided himself on precision. He wasn't a visionary like Nolan Scent, nor did he care to be. His strength lay in execution--turning grand ideas into reality, managing the details others overlooked, and ensuring nothing deviated from the plan. That was why Nolan trusted him. And why he was here.

From his office at Delta Precision Engineering, Lucas sifted through the latest performance metrics streaming in from Harmony Falls. The numbers were solid--efficiency gains, production outputs, and AI-assisted workflows all exceeding projections. Yet, beneath the glowing figures, the signs of strain were unmistakable.

Worker sentiment was dropping. Engagement scores flagged. Local businesses, once the backbone of the town's economy, were folding one by one, unable to compete. Harmony Falls was hanging by a thread--its residents caught between fear and exhaustion, their choices narrowing with each passing day.

Exactly as planned.

Lucas leaned back, satisfied. The town was transitioning--predictably, inevitably. Disruption was the necessary first step, and the next phase would offer the solution. He knew Nolan would be pleased, and that made the pressure to deliver all the sharper. He needed to get this data in front of him.

He glanced at a message from his team: "Local unrest indicators rising. Two more layoffs announced. ETA for non-Nolan company insolvency: 6 weeks." Perfect timing. The President, already under fire for his administration's inability to address the AI crisis, would soon have no choice but to listen.

Lucas closed the dashboard and hit send. Harmony Falls was a microcosm of the future. The only question was whether the world would embrace it willingly--or have it imposed.

*The asteroid didn't obliterate life on Earth instantly. It reshaped conditions, destabilizing ecosystems until the old ways could no longer survive. Harmony Falls mirrored that process, its people grappling with forces they didn't yet understand. The town was poised on the edge of a precipice, waiting for the tipping point that would seal its fate--and perhaps the fate of the entire nation.*

###

# CHAPTER 3

The sprawling glass facade of Scent Technologies HQ reflected the late afternoon sun as Molly Scent stepped out of her car. The building itself was a testament to her father's vision--cutting-edge architecture seamlessly blending technology and human ambition. Yet, as she approached the entrance, her thoughts drifted. Her father's directives always came with layers, and she wondered what lay beneath the surface of this particular tour.

Dr. Meredith Park, the overall lead for Project Heal, greeted her with a warm smile and an extended hand. "Ms. Scent, welcome. We're thrilled to have you here."
"Dr. Park," Molly said, shaking her hand firmly. "Thank you for arranging this."
"We've prepared a full tour of the key projects," Dr. Park said, leading Molly through the glass doors into a pristine lobby humming with quiet energy. "Project Heal is the culmination of decades of research, all focused on unlocking the potential of neural chip technology to revolutionize medicine."
Molly nodded, keeping her expression composed. She had been briefed on Project Heal before but had never seen its inner workings. Her father's insistence on this visit felt deliberate--as if he wanted her to understand just how much was at stake.

**Restoring Sight**
The first lab was sleek and sterile, lined with diagnostic stations and equipment. A researcher stood beside a table covered with sleek, biocompatible neural chips and a set of augmented-reality glasses.
"This is our Vision Restoration Program," Dr. Park explained. "We've developed BCI implants that bypass damaged optic nerves, transmitting visual data directly to the visual cortex."
Molly's gaze fell on the neural chips--thin, disc-like implants no

larger than a coin, designed to integrate seamlessly with brain tissue. A thin fiber-optic strand extended from each chip, allowing external connection via a small interface port placed at the base of the skull.
"These glasses work in tandem with the BCI to reconstruct an individual's sight," Dr. Park continued, gesturing toward a patient in her sixties. The woman put on the glasses, her eyes widening as she looked around the room.
"It's... incredible," she whispered. "I can see my hands. I can see you." She turned toward the researcher beside her. "I can see my granddaughter's face again."
Molly studied the woman, her emotions carefully guarded. "How scalable is this?"
"We're in the final stages of clinical trials," Dr. Park replied. "Once approved, millions of people could regain functional sight."

**Restoring Movement**

In the next lab, a group of paraplegic patients moved through carefully monitored exercises. Their limbs, once unresponsive, responded fluidly with the help of mechanical exoskeletons.
"Our Movement Restoration Program uses BCIs implanted in the motor cortex to bypass spinal cord damage," Dr. Park said. "Neural signals are re-routed, allowing direct brain-to-limb communication."
Molly watched as a young man, once confined to a wheelchair, took his first unaided steps. His legs trembled, but his expression burned with determination. The room burst into quiet applause.
Molly allowed herself a small nod. This was impressive.

**Memory Reconstruction**

In the third lab, rows of screens flickered with fragmented images--some grainy, others vividly reconstructed.
"This is our Memory Reconstruction Program," Dr. Park explained. "For patients suffering from Alzheimer's or traumatic brain injuries, we've developed an interface that retrieves, stabilizes, and, in some cases, rebuilds lost memories."
A researcher pulled up a patient's childhood memory--a grainy

black-and-white video of a boy playing in a backyard. The elderly patient, seated before the screen, gasped.

"I remember this..." His voice cracked. Tears welled in his eyes. "I thought it was gone forever."

Dr. Park turned to Molly. "It's more than memory restoration, Ms. Scent. It's about restoring identity."

**Emotional Regulation**

The final lab felt calmer--patients sat in reclining chairs wearing sleek neural headbands, their expressions serene.

"This is our Emotional Regulation Program," Dr. Park said. "Designed for patients with severe PTSD, depression, and anxiety, the BCI interacts with neural pathways to stabilize emotional responses."

A woman, once debilitated by trauma, now spoke with steady composure. "It's like a weight I didn't know I was carrying has been lifted."

Molly absorbed the scope of the projects. Each lab presented undeniable advancements--but all relied on one fundamental technology.

As they exited the lab, Molly turned to Dr. Park. "I noticed that every patient had an interface port on their neck. But the BCIs clearly interact with different parts of the brain. Why are they all in the same place?"

Dr. Park's expression flickered with quiet approval. "I'm impressed with your observation, Ms. Scent." She gestured toward a nearby schematic showing a cross-section of the neural chip system.

"The BCIs themselves are surgically implanted in different areas depending on their function--motor cortex, sensory cortex, prefrontal cortex, or brainstem. But the interface port--the point where the BCI connects externally--is standardized. As you would have seen, the ports glow when the BCI chips are active."

Molly studied the diagram of a thin fiber-optic cable running from the chip to a small, discreet port at the base of the skull.

The ports have been designed to optimize how we can deal with scaling to service large patient sets, for diagnostics, maintenance, upgrades, calibration of new implants. It ensures seamless external integration without requiring invasive procedures."

Molly let the information settle. The technology was elegant, efficient--and universal across all Project Heal patients.

Except for one.

"And Milo?" she asked.

Dr. Park's expression cooled slightly. "Milo's case is... unique."

"I'll let Dr. Numan update you on Project Milo."

Molly's expression remained calm, but a quiet pride stirred within her. The technology was extraordinary--far beyond what even she had expected. Emotional stability, restored memories, controlled movements--each breakthrough seemed like a lifeline to people who had thought hope was out of reach. Her father's vision was coming to life, and she was part of it. Scent Technologies wasn't just reshaping industries; it was reshaping lives. She thought about the families she'd met during the tour, their gratitude, their stories of transformation. What they were doing wasn't just innovation—it was a revolution. A better world wasn't just possible; it was being built, one neural connection at a time. Molly had always believed in her father's work, but now she saw the scope of what it could mean for humanity. For the first time, she felt the weight of her role not as a burden, but as a privilege. The future wasn't some distant dream—it was here, and she was ready to carry it forward.

#

The rooftop garden is an expansive oasis in the stark, metallic lines of Scent Laboratories. Planters filled with wildflowers and fruiting trees soften the edges of the city skyline. A subtle hum of drones in the distance blends with the sound of wind rustling through the greenery. Ethan Numan sits cross-legged on the ground near a low wall, his fingers brushing the leaves of a fragrant basil plant. He's absorbed in the rhythm of nature, but his sharp, analytical mind is elsewhere. The garden serves a dual purpose: it allows his twin brother Milo, who cannot leave their penthouse cum laboratory, to experience "being outside" safely. The setup is meticulous, designed to cater to Milo's needs, but it's also a place where Ethan finds his rare moments of calm. The penthouse itself, visible through the glass wall at the edge of the garden, is a marvel of design: wide, open spaces with subtle assistive technology integrated into every aspect to support Milo's limited mobility. For Ethan, this space is not just a home--it's a fortress where he has poured every ounce of himself into his work for Milo.

But the calm exterior doesn't tell the whole story. Ethan carries a weight: the knowledge of what he did to Milo before they were even born. He doesn't speak of it, but it defines everything about him. It's why his relationships are few, his social circle even smaller, and why he's spent years in near-isolation developing human-centric AI. If he can fix Milo--cure him--then maybe he can quiet that primal part of himself he despises. Nolan recognized this in Ethan the first time they met: the alpha instinct, buried under the surface but unmistakable. Ethan had hated him for it--hated that Nolan saw in him something he wished didn't exist. But Nolan also offered him something no one else could: a way to cure Milo.

That had been a year ago. Ethan and Milo had left their lives behind to move across the country into this purpose-built laboratory. To cure Milo. To create the future of human-AI. For Ethan, it wasn't a choice. He would have moved to the moon if it meant getting closer to the goal. Now, as the sunlight warms his face, Ethan glances at the time. He's expecting Molly Scent, Nolan's only child. He doesn't want to meet her, but he knows she's here to promote Project Heal, the initiative tied to his research. It's a chore, one he accepts grudgingly. He has little patience for interruptions, but he also knows better than to cross Nolan.

Ethan stands, brushing dirt off his hands. His posture is tall but unassuming--until you notice his eyes. They give away nothing. Ethan catches his reflection in the glass door as he steps back inside, his gaze flickering for a moment before settling into its usual inscrutable calm.

Dr. Park led Molly to a private elevator at the end of a long corridor. The sleek, silver doors reflected Molly's sharp features as she turned to the Project Heal lead. "This is where Professor Ethan Numan works," Dr. Park said, gesturing to the elevator. "He oversees one of our most ambitious projects, but he prefers to work in seclusion."

Molly raised an eyebrow. "Seclusion?" Dr. Park's smile was tight. "You'll understand when you meet him. He lives on-site with his twin brother." Molly stepped into the sleek glass elevator, the doors closing with a smooth hum. The ascent is quiet except for the faint rush of air. She's alone, but as the floors tick upward, she feels something--a faint brush against her cheek. Startled, she glances around, her hand reflexively reaching for her face. The sensation lingers, an almost imperceptible movement of air. She stiffens, staring at the empty space in front of her.

The elevator dings, and the doors slide open. Ethan is standing just outside, waiting for her. As Molly steps into the rooftop garden, the stark contrast between the sterile lab and this lush, vibrant space takes her by surprise. Ethan stands to the side, his arms crossed, watching her take it in. "Dr. Park didn't say you'd be giving a tour of the greenery," she says lightly, trying to match his cool demeanor. "It's not for show," Ethan replies. "It's for my brother." He gestures vaguely toward the penthouse. "He doesn't get out much." Molly tilts her head. "Milo?"

"My brother." Ethan hesitates, then adds, "You'll meet him later." There's a beat of silence. Molly studies Ethan, noting the sharp intelligence in his gaze but also the guardedness. He feels like the opposite of what she expected from someone working so closely with her father--a little rough around the edges, more like a reluctant genius than a corporate cog. "I hear you're here for Project Heal," Ethan says finally. "Big shoes to fill, promoting your father's latest masterpiece."

Molly raises an eyebrow. "You don't sound convinced." Ethan

smirks faintly. "Let's just say I prefer working on the project to talking about it."
"Can you at least tell me something about Project Milo, or better yet, maybe I could meet the infamous Milo."
Ethan guided Molly to a seating area surrounded by lush fauna.
"Milo is my twin brother. He suffered a lack of oxygen to the brain in the womb and as result he has an extreme case of locked-in syndrome. As far as we can tell his brain is functioning, but he is only capable of moving his eyes."
"And you've dedicated your life to finding a cure?" Ethan didn't answer Molly's question, moving on quickly, saying, "My studying neuroscience aligned with helping my brother, your father's organization provided limited funding for a number of years and access to the developments of Project Heal. What your father didn't know was what I was doing with quantum computing. When he found out, it took him 3 months to get Milo and I here and build me a lab, which I suspect is amongst the most advanced on the planet."

"What could you be doing that is more advanced than all the projects Dr. Park has just shown me?"
Before Ethan can answer Molly hears the soft whir of motors as Milo approaches from elsewhere in the garden. Molly's breath catches when she sees him: the striking resemblance to Ethan is unmistakable, but the differences are stark. Milo's body is motionless, confined to a state of physical stillness, but his eyes are extraordinary. They seem to hold a depth and vitality that contrasts sharply with Ethan's guarded, unreadable gaze. For a moment, Molly doesn't know what to say. Then Milo's eyes shift, locking onto hers with startling clarity. She feels as if he's seeing right through her, and the sensation leaves her momentarily disarmed.
"Don't stare," Ethan says lightly, breaking the silence. "He'll think you're trying to figure him out." Molly glances at Ethan, realizing the irony: Milo's eyes reveal everything, while Ethan's reveal nothing.

The transition from the verdant rooftop garden to the stark interior of the lab on the floor below was jarring. Molly stepped through the sleek, automatic doors into a cavernous space filled with glowing monitors, modular workstations, and rows of equipment humming softly with activity. Overhead, recessed lights cast a cold, clinical glow. But it was the centerpiece of the room that stopped her in her tracks: a massive quantum computer, its core encased in layers of polished chrome and glass, cables spilling out in intricate webs. A faint, otherworldly hum emanated from it, as if the machine itself was alive. Ethan glanced at her reaction, a smirk tugging at his lips. "Impressive, isn't it?" Molly's voice was barely above a whisper. "It looks like something out of a sci-fi movie." "Movies tend to undersell," Ethan said. He gestured toward the towering machine. "This is the heart of Project Milo. Every calculation, every decision, every ounce of data processed for him flows through this system."

Molly tore her eyes away from the machine to follow Ethan toward a side workstation. On the central monitor was a glowing, three-dimensional map of what she recognized as the human brain. Dozens of glowing nodes flickered across the image, each connected by dense networks of lines that pulsed faintly, like a living organism. Ethan tapped the monitor, and the image zoomed in, focusing on one of the smaller nodes. "This," he said, pointing to a glowing point on the map, "is what a typical Project Heal chip interacts with--a single neural pathway. Think of it like a country road: it's narrow, focused, and designed to reconnect small breaks in damaged neural circuits. It's revolutionary, but it's also limited. A Project Heal chip can guide movement in a hand, stabilize a tremor, or rebuild a basic memory connection. Small miracles."

He swiped his hand across the monitor, and the image zoomed out again to show the entire network of glowing nodes. "But Milo's brain? That's not a country road. It's a collapsed bridge in the middle of an Amazonian river system. His brain signals are so diffuse, so disrupted, that reconnecting a single pathway does nothing. We're not fixing roads--we're building an entire infrastructure." He tapped the screen again, highlighting several larger, brighter clusters. "These are the hubs we've mapped so far. Milo has over a dozen BCIs implanted across critical regions of his brain--motor cortex, sensory cortex, prefrontal cortex, even deep subcortical areas like the basal ganglia. Each one is essentially a node in a vast network, connected to this." He gestured toward the quantum computer.

Molly's brow furrowed. "Why does Milo need... that?" She nodded toward the quantum computer. "The Project Heal chips don't seem to need anything like it." Ethan leaned against the workstation, folding his arms. "Because the Project Heal chips are essentially problem solvers. They take known neural patterns and repair or guide them. They're brilliant, but they work within established pathways." He paused. "Milo doesn't have pathways. His brain is chaos. Years of atrophy and damage have scrambled his signals beyond recognition. What Project Heal can't do is create order out of chaos."

"That's where the quantum computer comes in?"

"Exactly. Think of Milo's brain like a flooding river: all that energy, all that potential, but it's uncontrolled. The quantum computer acts as a dam and a series of canals. It doesn't just process his brain signals--it predicts them, organizes them, and amplifies them. Each of Milo's BCIs collects raw data from his brain, sends it to the quantum computer for processing, and receives instructions in real time. Without this system, those BCIs would just be reading static."

Molly turned back to the monitor, watching the intricate neural network pulse and shift. "How many people could benefit from this kind of technology?" Ethan's jaw tightened slightly, and for a moment, she thought he might brush off the question. But then he said, "Not many. Not yet. This setup is entirely bespoke--designed for Milo's unique condition. And it's unsustainable. The quantum computer alone requires a level of energy and maintenance that makes it impossible to scale for widespread use. For now, it's not about curing the masses. It's about seeing if this can work for one person."

Ethan's gaze lingered on the monitor, where the glowing nodes continued to pulse. "Milo's been trapped in his own mind for as long as I can remember. He can hear us, understand us, but he can't respond. He can't move. Project Milo isn't just about giving him back control of his body--it's about giving him a voice. A way to tell me what he's been thinking all these years."

Molly's voice softened. "And you think it'll work?" Ethan didn't answer immediately. Instead, he stepped over to another console, where a second monitor displayed a live feed of Milo's neural activity. The patterns were erratic, chaotic--but there was a rhythm buried beneath the noise, faint and fragile.

Ethan didn't answer immediately. Instead, he led her to a secondary workstation, where a series of screens displayed a humanoid robotic avatar, sleek and functional, its movements surprisingly smooth as it lifted a cup from one side of the table and placed it on the other. Molly stared as the avatar repeated the movement, the precision almost eerie.

"That's Milo," Ethan said. Molly's breath caught. "What do you mean?"

He gestured toward the monitor. One of the screens displayed live neural activity mapped to the avatar's movements. "Right now, Milo is controlling that avatar. His BCIs are sending signals to the quantum computer, which decodes them and translates them into motor commands for the robot. The movements are basic for now, but they're entirely his."

Molly moved closer, watching as the avatar turned its head, its gaze oddly deliberate. "He's doing this?" Ethan nodded. "When we started, we could only pick up fragments--vague signals that hinted at intent. But now we're at the point where Milo can fully control the avatar's limbs, even grasp objects. It's the first time in his life he's been able to reach out and interact with the world."

Molly turned back to Ethan, her expression a mix of awe and

curiosity. "What's the next step?"
"The exoskeleton," Ethan replied without hesitation. "The avatar is a proxy, but the goal is to reconnect Milo to his own body. The exoskeleton will interface directly with his muscles, bypassing his damaged nervous system entirely. It's a monumental challenge--his body has been paralyzed for so long; we'll have to retrain his muscles to work with the signals. But we'll get there." Molly's gaze shifted to another part of the lab, where a prototype of the exoskeleton stood. It was sleek and skeletal, a blend of lightweight alloys and soft robotics. Even at rest, it looked like it was waiting to come alive.
"And after that?" she asked. Ethan hesitated for the first time. "After that... who knows? If we can rebuild Milo's body, if we can fully reconnect his mind to the world, then there's no limit to what this technology can do. Not just for him--for everyone." Ethan gestured toward the quantum computer again. "Project Heal is about helping people function. Project Milo is about something bigger: redefining the relationship between the brain and the body. If we can crack this--if we can make this work--then there's no limit to what we can do."
Molly glanced back at Milo's feed on the monitor, then at Ethan. "And if you don't?"
Ethan's expression hardened. "Failure isn't an option." As they spoke, the avatar raised a hand, the movement slow but deliberate. Milo's gaze--alive and unyielding--flickered on the monitor. For the first time, Molly thought she understood the weight of Ethan's words. This wasn't just a project. It was a lifeline, a gamble on something bigger than technology--a belief that even the most broken bridges could be rebuilt.
Molly looked from the avatar to the huge quantum computer and then to Milo's broken form in the wheelchair connected via BCI's to the most powerful quantum computer on the planet. She wondered why anyone would want to speak against this work. What could be more valuable than all the things she had seen today. Why were people so scared of technology? Even with this super

powerful computer it was still Milo in control. Project Heal and Project Milo energized her in a way she hadn't expected. She was excited for her dinner appointment later that evening with Professor Jansen.

# STAGE 2: DUST CLOUDS – DISLOCATION OF LABOR

## Stage 2: Dust Clouds – Dislocation of Labor (macro view)

The dust clouds did not settle—they thickened.
The asteroid's impact was sudden—but the collapse that followed was slower and more painful. AI's initial shockwave was manageable, even promising. Companies boasted record productivity, investors celebrated surging valuations. AI wasn't replacing entire industries—it was "optimizing" them.

But soon, the human cost became undeniable.

By 2026, AI-driven automation displaced large portions of the manufacturing workforce. AI-coordinated supply chains no longer needed drivers when self-driving fleets took over. Warehouses, once dependent on thousands of human workers, functioned flawlessly with robotic systems.

The shift wasn't gradual. It was a landslide.

"AI-driven automation has accelerated job displacement faster than any prior technological shift," industry analysts noted in 2026. (McKinsey, 2026)

**The Economic Fallout**
Entire communities—towns built around industrial hubs—found themselves in economic freefall.

In the American Midwest, AI adoption in manufacturing hubs caused regional economic strain, driving unemployment toward levels not seen since the Great Depression. (MIT Sloan, 2024)

"The regional economic divide has widened dramatically," Pew Research warned in 2027. "The ripple effects of AI displacement are disproportionately concentrated in working-class communities." (Pew Research, 2027)

The AI skill gap became an insurmountable barrier. While demand for AI specialists surged, only 2% of displaced workers had the qualifications to transition. (McKinsey, 2025)

- Truck drivers were replaced by AI-guided fleets.
- Warehouse staff were made redundant by self-organizing AI logistics systems.
- Manufacturing lines were automated at a pace no human workforce could match.

**Social Disruption**

Between 2025 and 2027, labor unrest increased sharply—a desperate, last stand against forces too large to fight.

"AI-driven job loss has fueled the largest wave of organized labor action in decades," The Guardian reported in 2026. (The Guardian, 2026)

Mass protests erupted globally as AI-driven companies posted record profits while unemployment rates spiraled upward.

Governments scrambled to respond—but policy moved too slowly. For every job lost, AI created new efficiencies—but the displaced weren't the ones benefiting.

"We are not moving fast enough to regulate AI," The Guardian noted. "Corporations are outpacing policy by orders of magnitude." (The Guardian, 2026)

**The Dust Did Not Settle**

It was thickening.

And for millions, the way forward was no longer visible.

### ***Stage 2: Dust Clouds - Dislocation of Labor (micro view)***

*The single bare bulb hanging from the kitchen ceiling flickered faintly, casting uneven shadows across the cramped room. Jim Whelan sat at the table, his hands clasped around a coffee mug that had long gone cold. The sink was piled with dishes, but the silence was heavier than the mess. He stared at the envelope in front of him, the logo of General Freight Solutions stamped in the corner.*

*Three weeks ago, the layoffs had been announced. The whispers had started long before that--rumors of AI logistics software, of automated dispatchers, of self-driving trucks. But rumors were just that, and Jim had told himself they wouldn't reach him. He was too experienced. Too essential. The letter proved otherwise.*

*Jim rubbed a hand over his face, the callouses rough against his skin. He wasn't a man who just moved boxes. He was the guy who made sure things got where they needed to go. The quiet backbone of a supply chain that had always needed human hands--until now.*

*AI didn't need sleep. It didn't take breaks. It didn't get distracted on long drives or call in sick. It didn't make mistakes.*

*A faint murmur drifted in from the next room. Karen was watching one of her home renovation shows again. She used to comment on them, talk about which designs she liked, which ones she thought were impractical. Now, she barely spoke. She'd gone back to waitressing at the diner, but it wasn't enough. They had two boys in college. He hadn't told them yet.*

*His eyes drifted to the corner of the room, where a stack of unopened bills sat. His severance check would barely cover the next few months. The life insurance policy, on the other hand...*

*Jim clenched his jaw, forcing the thought away. It wasn't running away. It was making sure Karen and the boys had a future.*

*Laughter. Karen's laugh. Sharp, sudden, unexpected. Jim froze. It had been weeks since he'd heard it. The sound cut through him like a knife. The chair scraped against the floor as he stood abruptly. The envelope slipped from his fingers, landing on the table, forgotten. He stepped out onto the porch, inhaling the cool night air. Harmony Falls had always been quiet, but now, it felt different. Empty. Hollow. Like the town was holding its breath.*

*Above him, the sky stretched wide and indifferent, the stars scattered across the dark expanse. Did it even matter, in the grand scheme of things, if men like him disappeared? The screen door creaked. Jim turned to see Karen standing there, a dishtowel in her hand, concern etched into her face. "Jim?" she asked softly. "What's wrong?"*

*He forced a smile. "Nothing. Just getting some air." She lingered, studying him, but didn't push. Instead, she nodded and disappeared back inside.*

*Jim stayed where he was, staring up at the sky.*

*The asteroid hadn't wiped everything out in an instant. It was slow. Creeping. A force that spread, unrelenting. Somewhere deep in his gut, Jim knew this wasn't just happening to him. It wasn't just Harmony Falls. AI was spreading--drifting on the winds of progress like fine dust. And the world was still breathing it in.*

# CHAPTER 4

The private conference room in the penthouse of Nolan Scent's Silicon Valley headquarters was a study in understated luxury. Floor-to-ceiling windows revealed a commanding view of the Bay Area, its tech hubs glinting like modern-day fortresses. The table, a single slab of polished black granite, stretched the length of the room, seating a dozen of the most powerful individuals in America.

They represented the elite of the elite: a Wall Street titan whose firm controlled trillions in assets, the CEO of a major pharmaceutical conglomerate, a media mogul whose networks shaped public opinion, and several others from industries that had thrived under the old systems. Each one had weathered disruptions before--market crashes, political upheavals, technological shifts--but the speed and scale of the AI revolution had shaken even their ironclad confidence.

These were people accustomed to control, and the uncertainty AI had unleashed was threatening their grip. Labor strikes were spreading. Their own industries were scrambling to adapt. Public anger at the growing chasm between the haves and have-nots was becoming harder to ignore. For the first time, they felt the ground beneath their feet tremble.

Nolan Scent stood at the head of the table, the only one in the room with the poise of someone completely at ease. He had summoned them here not to discuss problems but to present solutions--his solutions.

"Thank you all for coming," Nolan began, his voice calm but commanding. "I know you're under pressure--protests outside your offices, supply chains disrupted, regulators hovering like vultures. The world feels like it's slipping out of control. And if you're anything like me, you've been asking yourself one question: how do we fix this?"

He didn't wait for a response. With a click of the remote in his hand, the screen behind him lit up, displaying an aerial view of Harmony Falls. "This," Nolan said, gesturing to the idyllic scene, "is Harmony Falls. A small town, no different from thousands of others across America. A place where AI-driven efficiencies have displaced jobs faster than anyone could have imagined."

"But in Harmony Falls," he continued, clicking the remote once more, "something different is happening."

The screen shifted to show images of Project Heal, Scent Technologies' flagship initiative. Patients were walking for the first time in decades, neurological disorders were being reversed, children were playing under the watchful eye of doctors who praised the technology.

"Project Heal," Nolan said, "isn't just a medical program--it's a lifeline. It's proof of what AI can do when it's directed toward human progress. The neural chips we've developed have given people back their lives. They've turned impossible dreams into everyday realities."

The attendees nodded, some grudgingly, others with genuine approval. Even the harshest critics of Nolan's AI had to admit that Project Heal's public success was undeniable.

Nolan's tone shifted slightly, becoming more pointed. "But it's not just about healing individuals. It's about healing communities." The screen now showed footage from within one of Nolan's Harmony Falls factories. Workers moved efficiently, assembling products with smooth precision. They smiled as they worked, their demeanor calm and focused. It wasn't the weary resignation seen in factories of the past--it was something else, something harder to define.

"These workers," Nolan said, "were part of the displaced. They'd lost their jobs, their purpose, their stability. But through AI-guided programs, they've been re-skilled and repurposed for a modern workforce." He let the phrase hang for a moment before continuing. "It's not the kind of work they used to do, but they've embraced it. They're thriving, as you can see. The community is rebuilding itself." The screen showed further examples: former office workers now sorting materials in recycling centers; laid-off machinists running logistics for drone deliveries; community gardens flourishing with volunteers who seemed genuinely happy to be planting and harvesting crops.

"It's simple," Nolan said. "Where there's no hope, we give it back. Where there's chaos, we create order."

What Nolan didn't say--and what no one outside his inner circle could know--was that this transformation wasn't the result of some miraculous re-skilling program. The neural chips that had been introduced "for free" to aid workers in adapting to new roles did far more than improve productivity. They shaped emotions, dulled dissatisfaction, and rewired ambition. Workers who would have bristled at being relegated to menial tasks now took pride in them. The unemployed, instead of revolting, found themselves content to help in whatever way they could.

The chips weren't marketed as control devices--they were sold as tools for focus, stress reduction, and emotional stability. And in a world teetering on the brink of collapse, no one questioned the fine print.

As the screen faded to black, Nolan turned back to the room. The group stared at him, some intrigued, others skeptical.

"So, you've made Harmony Falls look like a corporate paradise," one of the attendees said, his tone biting. "But what about the rest of us? Our towns aren't Harmony Falls. We're dealing with protests, strikes, and regulators breathing down our necks. Where's your re-skilling program for the rest of the country?"

Nolan raised a hand to stop the barrage before it could start. "Harmony Falls isn't just a success story. It's a prototype. A proof of concept. If it works there, it can work anywhere. But I need time to scale it up."

"And the regulators?" another attendee pressed. "You think they'll let you roll out these programs without tearing you apart first?"

A faint smile tugged at the corner of Nolan's lips. "I'll handle the regulators. More specifically, I'll handle the President."

Nolan leaned forward, his voice dropping just enough to make everyone listen. "Here's the reality. The President is under as much pressure as we are--maybe more. He knows the protests are a ticking time bomb, and he doesn't have a solution. No one does. Except us."

He let the statement hang for a moment before continuing. "Give me one month. In one month, Harmony Falls will prove that this system works. The regulators will see the results. The President will see the results. And when I show him what's possible, he won't just approve it--he'll make sure we're untouchable."

Nolan straightened, his gaze sweeping the room. "I understand your frustrations. But what I'm building isn't just a solution for Harmony Falls--it's the future. A future where we control the narrative, the workforce, and the outcomes. It's not about managing the chaos. It's about ending it."

The room was silent, the weight of his words settling over them. One by one, the attendees began to nod, some reluctantly, others with growing confidence. Nolan had given them what they needed: a promise, a plan, and the assurance that the 1% would remain on top.

As the meeting ended and the attendees filtered out, Nolan lingered, gazing at the darkened screen. Harmony Falls wasn't just a prototype--it was the foundation of a world he was quietly, methodically remaking. One chip at a time.

##

# CHAPTER 5

**M**olly had chosen the restaurant for its seclusion, not its reputation, though it had plenty of that too. The maître d' had ushered her and Professor Jansen to a discreet corner table as soon as they arrived, bypassing the bustle of the main dining room. Soft lighting cast a warm glow over their table, the murmur of distant conversations muffled by thick carpcts and acoustic design.

Jansen took his seat, his eyes scanning the room with mild curiosity. "I have to admit," he said, folding his napkin over his lap, "this is a bit more polished than I imagined for someone as young as you."

Molly gave him a faint smile, unfazed. "I like privacy when I eat. And the chef here is very accommodating."

Jansen raised an eyebrow. "Accommodating?"

"I have dietary restrictions," Molly said simply, waving away the explanation. "He works around them. Plus, he knows how to keep things off social media. I'd rather not see my dinner plastered on some influencer's page."

"Fair enough," Jansen said, settling back into his chair. "So, what's good here?"

"Whatever I feel like," Molly replied with a playful smirk. "The chef will even bring in takeout pizza if I ask."

Jansen chuckled, though his expression remained skeptical. "That sounds... inconvenient for him."

"For me, it's convenient," Molly countered, leaning back. She didn't mind the small talk, but she hadn't invited him for that. "So, Professor, how do you feel about AI saving humanity?"

Jansen tilted his head, as though considering the question. "Depends on your definition of 'saving.' I imagine you have one ready."

"Preventing unnecessary suffering, curing diseases, improving lives," Molly said, her tone brisk. "You know, the things science is supposed to do."

Jansen smiled faintly. "And you think AI will do all that?"

"It's already happening," Molly said, leaning forward slightly. "You saw the news on Project Heal, didn't you? AI-guided BCIs restoring sight to the blind, helping stroke patients regain movement. The possibilities are endless."

Jansen nodded slowly, his expression thoughtful. "Impressive, no doubt. But don't you think—"

Molly cut him off, her voice gaining an edge. "What I don't think, Professor, is that your alarmist comparisons to prehistoric extinction events help the conversation."

Jansen blinked, then laughed softly, surprising her. "You're very direct."

Molly didn't flinch. "I'm serious. You're a man of science. How can you call AI an extinction-level event? That kind of language is irresponsible."

Jansen's smile faded, and he picked up his water glass, swirling the liquid idly. "Irresponsible, or inconvenient?"

Molly tilted her head, her expression sharpening. "I invited you here for a conversation, not a debate."

"And yet here we are," Jansen said evenly. "Tell me something, Ms. Scent, have you really considered what it means to implant semi-sentient chips into humans? To integrate something with the potential to learn, adapt, and evolve into our very biology?"

Molly didn't hesitate. "Of course I have. That's the point of Project Heal. We're giving people their lives back."

"And who controls the chips?" Jansen asked quietly.

Molly frowned. "The chips are tools. They don't need to be 'controlled.' They work within parameters set by their programming."

"Ah, parameters," Jansen said, his tone soft but probing. "And who sets those parameters? What happens when those parameters evolve, or—more likely—when someone decides to change them?"

Molly's jaw tightened. "We're not building Skynet, Professor. These chips are designed to help people, not hurt them."

"That's what fire was for too," Jansen said with a faint smile.

"Cooking, warmth, protection. But we both know fire isn't just a tool—it's power. And power is rarely left in the hands of those who use it wisely."

Molly narrowed her eyes, studying him for a moment. She decided it was time to shift the focus. "What about you?" she asked. "I've read some of your work—enough to know you've touched on near-death experiences. Not the most rigorous area of study for someone in your field."

Jansen's expression remained neutral. "Science is about exploration. Dismissing a phenomenon simply because it doesn't fit neatly into a framework isn't science—it's arrogance."

"So, you believe in souls, then?" Molly asked, her tone laced with skepticism. "In lights at the end of tunnels? Loved ones waiting on the other side?"

Jansen leaned forward slightly, his gaze steady. "I believe there's more to life—and death—than we understand. And I believe dismissing something because it sounds 'wishy-washy,' as you put it, limits us as scientists."

Molly smirked. "That's a very poetic answer."

"Poetry and science aren't mutually exclusive," Jansen replied, his tone unruffled. "But tell me—why the sudden interest in my views on NDEs?"

Molly hesitated, not wanting to reveal too much. "I'm just curious how someone so grounded in prehistoric facts can entertain something so abstract."

Jansen leaned back, folding his hands. "And I'm curious how someone so committed to the future can be so dismissive of the past. If we're talking about extinction events, it's worth considering what makes humanity worth saving in the first place."

Molly shifted uncomfortably in her seat, the conversation veering further off course than she intended. She cleared her throat, adopting a lighter tone. "You know, you'd probably find Project Heal fascinating. Why don't you come and see it for yourself?"

Jansen raised an eyebrow. "Are you extending an olive branch, or looking for ammunition to undermine me?"

Molly's smile was tight. "Maybe both."

Jansen chuckled. "I appreciate the offer. And while I'm sure what you're doing there is extraordinary, I'm more interested in what you're not showing the world."

Molly's gaze sharpened, but she kept her tone measured. "What's that supposed to mean?"

Jansen's expression was unreadable. "Let's just say I've seen enough revolutions in history to know they rarely come without a cost. But I'll think about your invitation."

The conversation paused as their meals arrived, the chef himself setting down Molly's meticulously prepared dish. Jansen glanced at it, then at his own simpler plate. "You're really trying to impress me, aren't you?"

Molly smirked. "Not even a little."

For a moment, they both laughed, the tension easing slightly. But as the meal continued, the questions lingered in the air, unanswered, hanging between them like a challenge neither was willing to fully address—yet.

Molly's fork hovered over her plate, forgotten as she launched into an enthusiastic recounting of Project Milo. Her eyes sparkled with the kind of passion that only came from genuine belief.

"It's just extraordinary," she said, her voice rising slightly as she gestured animatedly. "Ethan's work isn't just about curing his brother—it's about redefining what's possible. Milo isn't just locked in his body; he's essentially been locked out of the world. And now? He's moving. He's *communicating*. Do you understand what that means, Professor? It's... it's like opening a door that's been shut for someone their entire life."

Jansen nodded politely, watching her with a faint smile. She wasn't asking for his agreement—she was swept up in her own words, oblivious to his silence.

"And Project Heal—it's the same. Every chip, every breakthrough is giving people their lives back. My father's vision isn't just science fiction—it's here, now. People are walking again, seeing again, *living* again. I've seen it with my own eyes. And for Milo? It's only' the

beginning."
Her voice' softened, taking on a more reverent tone. "When I saw Milo control the avatar... I can't even describe it. The precision, the way his eyes lit up. It wasn't just movement—it was freedom. And Ethan... he's so driven, so brilliant. He's doing this for his brother, yes, but it's bigger than that. It's for everyone."
Jansen's gaze drifted slightly, her words fading into the background as his mind wandered to the faces of his daughters. He could almost see them—smiling, full of life, their eyes wide with the same enthusiasm Molly now radiated. He pictured his oldest, Lily, who would have been just a little younger than Molly now. Would she have been like this? Bright, hopeful, her heart swelling with the promise of this new world? For a moment, his chest tightened with the ache of what could never be. But strangely, Molly's enthusiasm didn't irritate him. It warmed him, her belief infectious in a way he didn't expect.
"Do you ever think," he interrupted softly, "about what all of this could mean? Beyond the breakthroughs, the successes. Do you ever think about what we lose in chasing what we gain?"
Molly frowned, her rhythm faltering. "What do you mean?"
Jansen leaned back, his expression a mix of thoughtfulness and sorrow. "It's just... you remind me of someone I lost. Someone who might have grown up to see this future you're so excited about." He paused, choosing his words carefully. "And maybe, if they'd had a chance to live, I'd feel the way you do about it. Enthusiastic. Hopeful."
Molly's expression softened, but Jansen didn't give her a chance to speak. His tone shifted slightly, sharpening like a blade in velvet.
"Progress is never free, Molly. It comes with a cost—one often hidden in the shadows of ambition. You see Milo as a miracle—and maybe he is. But who decides what's done with that miracle? Who gets to wield it?"
Molly's confidence faltered, though she forced herself to hold his gaze. "I've thought about that," she said quietly. "Maybe not as much as I should. That's why I wanted to talk to you."

Jansen's faint smile was almost kind. "And I appreciate the invitation. Though I suspect you had another motive."
Molly hesitated before leaning forward slightly, as if testing the waters. "I have to ask—I've seen references to near-death experiences in your work."
Jansen tilted his head, amusement flickering behind his weary eyes. "So, you *do* have a file on me."
She looked sheepish. "I skimmed it. Honestly, I haven't had time to go through it in detail."
"Clearly," Jansen said dryly, refilling his water glass. "Because if you had, you'd know my near-death experience happened at the bottom of a sinkhole. The same sinkhole that claimed the lives of my wife and two daughters."
The color drained from Molly's face just as the waiter set down dessert, bright cherry sauce pooling on the pristine plate. She stammered, her voice barely audible. "I... I didn't mean—"
Jansen raised a hand, cutting her off gently. "You didn't know. There's nothing to apologize for."
Molly looked down, shame flickering across her features.
Jansen's voice softened, though it carried the weight of grief. "I don't know what I experienced down there. Maybe it was a hallucination, like the models your AI builds—neural noise from a brain dealing with trauma. Or maybe it was something else entirely. All I know is that it felt *real.* Real enough to make me question everything I thought I understood."
The candle flame in the center of the table flickered, dancing in the silence.
"A physicist will tell you consciousness is just neurons firing, subatomic particles behaving according to laws—some known, some not. A priest will tell you the 'I' of your mind is a soul that persists somewhere beyond the body. I can't say who's right. All I know is that when I was pinned under that rubble, trapped between alive and dead, I felt something. Something that can't be reduced to atoms or biology."
Molly met his gaze, uncertain now. "And what did you experience?"

Jansen's eyes drifted to the candle, watching it burn as though it might hold the answer. "I was in and out of consciousness. I knew my family was buried under those boulders just a few feet from me, but we communicated when it should have been impossible. I can't explain it, but... I *felt* them. At the end, I felt them leave."

The flickering light seemed to dance on his face, catching the weariness carved into the lines around his eyes.

"Isn't it more likely that was in your head?" Molly asked carefully. "Your brain trying to make sense of extreme trauma?"

"Yes," Jansen replied without hesitation. "That's thc most reasonable explanation." He paused, considering his water glass. "But it doesn't satisfy me. It was the most vivid experience of my life, Molly. Something that transcended reason."

He lifted the glass, studying it as though" seeing something she couldn't. "No matter how thirsty you are—no matter that drinking this water could save your life—I can't drink enough to give *you* even the smallest drop."

Molly frowned, not understanding. "What does that mean?"

Jansen set the glass down gently, his tone quiet but firm. "Some things you have to experience for yourself. You can't be told or shown. That's what I felt at the bottom of that hole: something that makes me believe there's more to us than wires, circuits, and algorithms. Which is why I say... tread carefully. You don't put chips into people's heads without extreme caution."

Molly hesitated. "What makes you think precautions aren't being taken?"

Jansen held her gaze, unflinching. "Because people, Molly, aren't as good as we like to think we are."

Her mouth opened slightly, but no words came. For the first time that evening, her confidence wavered. Jansen gave her a moment before breaking the silence. "I'll come and see Project Heal," he said lightly, as if they'd been discussing nothing more serious than the weather.

Molly looked up, visibly relieved. "You will?"

"I will," he nodded, before adding with quiet authority, "But I have

a condition."
Her relief faltered. "What's that?"
"Take me to Harmony Falls as well."
Molly blinked, her face shifting as though searching for an objection. She found none. "Okay," she said finally, nodding. "I can do that."
"Good," Jansen said, the tension breaking just enough for him to spear a bite of dessert. "Now tell me—does the chef here do takeout pizza for everyone, or just you?"
Molly laughed despite herself, the sound breaking through the heaviness of the conversation. But even as they finished their meal, her smile faded with the memory of Jansen's words. She couldn't shake the weight of his story—or the flicker of doubt now lodged in the back of her mind.

#

The sound of the automated feeder hummed softly in the quiet of the dining room. Ethan sat across from Milo, who was reclined in his custom chair. The tube running from the feeder to Milo's mouth delivered an unappetizing greyish mush, while Ethan twirled spaghetti on his fork.
"You'd think they could make the stuff look less like it came from the bottom of a swamp," Ethan muttered, glancing at Milo's feeder with a wince. "But hey, at least it's packed with nutrients, right?"
Milo's eyes flicked toward Ethan, the faintest glimmer of amusement--or so Ethan liked to imagine.
Ethan sighed and leaned back in his chair, pushing his plate away. "So... Molly," he began, his tone half-conversational, half-uncertain.
Milo's gaze sharpened, those vivid eyes fixed on Ethan with unyielding intensity.
"She's... interesting," Ethan continued, twirling the fork absently. "Sharp. Confident. Maybe a little too confident." He smirked at the memory of Molly walking through the lab earlier, her questions coming rapid-fire, her energy almost infectious. "But she's not what

I expected. I thought she'd be--"
He hesitated, searching for the right word.
"--corporate," he said finally, waving his hand in a vague gesture. "You know, polished, fake-smile, PR spin type. But she's... human. She seems like she actually cares. And that laugh..."
Ethan trailed off, his expression softening as he stared at his plate. "It's... nice."
Milo's eyes narrowed slightly, as though scrutinizing him.
Ethan caught the look and huffed, defensive. "What? I'm just saying she's different. That's all." He paused, then added, almost to himself, "It's not like I like her or anything. I mean, okay, I like her, but not like that. You know?"
Milo's gaze didn't waver.
Ethan threw up his hands. "Why am I even talking to you about this? It's not like you--" He stopped himself, the words catching in his throat. "I mean, I don't even know if you care about stuff like that."
For a moment, Ethan stared at Milo, as if willing his brother to respond. Milo's expressive eyes softened, their intensity giving way to something gentler.
Ethan leaned forward, his voice quieter now. "But you do, don't you? You see things, feel things. Sometimes I wonder if you understand more than I do. About everything."
Milo blinked slowly, and for a second, Ethan thought he saw something--recognition, maybe even empathy.
Then, without warning, Milo's chair whirred to life.
The sudden movement startled Ethan. He frowned as Milo turned sharply away, his chair gliding toward the lab door.
"Seriously?" Ethan called after him, half-offended. "I'm pouring my heart out here, and you just... leave? Nice, Milo. Real nice."
Despite his irritation, Ethan got up and followed. "Where are you going, anyway?"
Milo's chair moved with purpose, entering the lab and stopping at the interface station.
Ethan's irritation faded into curiosity. "Oh, I see. You've got

something to say now?"

Milo's chair positioned itself under the connection port, and Ethan sighed, stepping forward to attach the interface. Within moments, Milo was online, his neural pathways synced with the lab's avatar system.

The avatar--a sleek humanoid robot with Milo's expressive eyes replicated on its face--activated and stepped forward. Ethan folded his arms, watching as Milo took control.

"What is it, little brother? You're clearly dying to tell me something."

The avatar paused, then dramatically raised one robotic hand to its metallic chest, as if clutching an invisible heart. With exaggerated flair, it tilted its head toward Ethan and extended its other hand outward, mimicking a romantic gesture.

Ethan blinked, confused. "What are you--"

The avatar pointed at Ethan, then pantomimed a beating heart, before gesturing dramatically toward an invisible figure Ethan could only assume was meant to be Molly.

Ethan froze, realization dawning. "Oh, no. No, no, no." He pointed at the avatar. "Don't even start."

The avatar placed its hands together as if in prayer, then tilted its head with mock adoration.

Ethan groaned, his cheeks flushing. "Come on, Milo. You're being ridiculous."

The avatar shrugged and pointed at Ethan again, this time making an exaggerated kissing motion.

Ethan couldn't help it--he laughed. "You're impossible. Likes, maybe. Okay? Likes. Not love. Let's not get carried away."

The avatar tilted its head, crossing its arms, clearly unconvinced.

Ethan shook his head, smiling despite himself. "I swear, you've got the emotional range of a rom-com protagonist in there. You know that?"

The avatar extended a hand, clapping Ethan lightly on the shoulder. It wasn't just playful; it was affectionate.

Ethan sighed, his tone softening. "Okay, fine. I like her. Happy?"

The avatar nodded once, decisively.
Ethan rolled his eyes, laughing again. "You're the worst, you know that?"
Milo's avatar leaned forward slightly, placing a hand over its metallic chest once more in mock sincerity, and Ethan laughed harder. "Yeah, yeah, message received."
The avatar turned and walked away, its metallic gait oddly triumphant, leaving Ethan alone in the lab.
Ethan watched it go, shaking his head. "You're lucky I love you, you know."

##

# CHAPTER 6

**M**artin Cole sat in the break-room of Delta Precision Manufacturing, a plastic coffee cup cradled in his hands. Around him, his coworkers murmured in low voices, the tension in the room thick enough to cut. The AI workshops from earlier that week had left everyone shaken.

Delta's management had outlined their plans with corporate polish, but the message was clear: automation was coming, and it was coming fast. Machines would take over the precision assembly lines. Most workers would no longer be needed in their current roles. There would be *opportunities* for re-skilling, the presenters had assured them--manual labor positions, cleaning, maintenance, or jobs at affiliated businesses outside Delta. But for seasoned workers like Martin, it felt more like a demotion than a new opportunity.

"What are we supposed to do?" one of his coworkers muttered. "I've been doing this job for twenty years. You think I'm gonna scrub floors now?"

Another chimed in, his voice laced with bitterness. "They're just shuffling us out the door without calling it a layoff."

Martin stayed silent, his gaze fixed on the coffee swirling in his cup. He shared their anger, their worry. At 45, with two teenagers at home and a mortgage he could barely keep up with, the thought of starting over in a menial job was crushing. But what choice did he have? The machines didn't call in sick, didn't need breaks, didn't complain. They were faster, cheaper, better.

A week later, Martin was called into a meeting with HR. The room was stark, its only decoration a motivational poster about adaptability hanging crookedly on the wall. Across the table sat a sleek, smiling consultant from Scent Technologies.

"Mr. Cole," the woman began, her voice warm but professional. "I understand you've expressed some concerns about the upcoming transitions at Delta."

Martin shifted in his seat, his jaw tightening. "Yeah, you could say that."

The consultant nodded, her expression sympathetic. "I completely understand. Change is hard, especially in industries like this. That's why we're offering a new program to help ease the transition. It's called the Human Augmentation Initiative, or HAI for short."

Martin frowned. "Augmentation? What's that supposed to mean?"

"It's a simple, non-invasive procedure," she explained, "where a small neural chip is implanted to enhance your cognitive adaptability and emotional resilience. It helps individuals adjust to new roles and responsibilities, reducing stress and improving satisfaction."

Martin snorted. "So, what--you put a chip in my head, and suddenly I'm okay with scrubbing toilets?"

The consultant didn't flinch. "It's not about making you 'okay' with anything. It's about giving you the tools to succeed in whatever role you take on. Think of it as levelling the playing field between you and the advanced systems being introduced."

Martin leaned back in his chair, crossing his arms. "And if I say no?"

The consultant's smile didn't waver, but her tone cooled slightly. "Of course, participation is voluntary. But I'd encourage you to consider the benefits carefully. Employees who choose not to participate may find the transition process more challenging."

A month later, Martin sat in another meeting room at Delta, this time for his re-skilling interview. The neural chip had been inserted two weeks earlier, and he had to admit--it was working. He felt calmer, more focused. The anxiety that had kept him awake at night, gnawing at the edges of his thoughts, was gone. He still wasn't thrilled about the idea of a manual labor role, but the frustration and resentment he'd felt before seemed distant, like a storm that had passed.

The HR manager across from him smiled warmly. "Mr. Cole, I see you've been flagged as an excellent candidate for our maintenance team. It's a hands-on role with a lot of variety, and I think you'd do very well in it."

Martin nodded slowly. "That sounds... good," he said, surprising even himself with the ease of his response. A month ago, he would have balked at the idea. Now, it seemed reasonable. Practical.

"I'm glad to hear that," the manager said. "And just so you know, this isn't the end of your journey. There are always opportunities to move up once you're settled into your new role."

Martin nodded again, his mind already shifting to practical concerns: learning the ropes, adjusting to the schedule, doing the best he could. It all felt... manageable. For the first time in months, he felt like he had a plan.

That evening, Martin sat at the kitchen table with his wife, explaining the new role. "It's not what I was doing before," he said, "but it's a good job. Steady hours, decent pay. We'll be fine."

His wife smiled, relief washing over her features. "That's great, Martin. I was so worried."

Martin smiled back, his thoughts already moving to his first day in the new role. The nagging doubts that had once plagued him seemed almost laughable now. The chip hadn't just helped him adapt--it had made him *content.* And for that, he was grateful.

*For Martin Cole, the asteroid didn't arrive in a flash of light or a crash of fire. It came in the form of a quiet shift, a subtle realignment of expectations. Life wasn't perfect, but it worked. And as the machines took over, as the town changed around him, Martin barely noticed the pieces of himself that were slipping away.*

# STAGE 3: DISRUPTION OF ECOSYSTEMS – AI EXPANSION

## Stage 3: Disruption of Ecosystems – AI Expansion (macro view)

The dust had not yet settled—but the eruptions had already begun.
AI was no longer a tool—it was an unstoppable force, reshaping industries, communities, and economies at a scale no policy or resistance could contain. Entire professions vanished. Power consolidated at the highest levels. The world wasn't recovering—it was being restructured.

The promises of AI efficiency and progress masked the true cost: an economic and societal upheaval that rewrote the fundamental balance of power. The few who controlled AI were no longer business leaders or politicians—they were engineers and algorithm architects. The creators had become the rulers.

**Healthcare: Automation Over Compassion**
By 2027, AI diagnostic systems had displaced a significant share of radiologists, while virtual health assistants replaced many general practitioners in urban centers. The shift was framed as progress—faster, more efficient, more accurate. But in reality, it was a numbers game.

Patients received quicker diagnoses but fewer second opinions. Treatment plans were optimized for cost-effectiveness, not human care. Rural and low-income patients were left behind, unable to access AI-driven premium services controlled by private healthcare conglomerates.

"AI-driven healthcare has increased speed and efficiency—but at the expense of patient care," the International Monetary Fund warned. (IMF, 2024)

By 2027, healthcare was no longer rationed by skill or availability —it was rationed by access to the right algorithm. (Brookings, 2024)

The divide wasn't just financial—it was existential. Healthcare had become another algorithmic privilege.

**Education: The Disintegration of Public Schools**

AI-driven learning platforms promised personalized education, accessible anytime, anywhere. But in practice, human teachers became a luxury.

By 2026, public schools in economically disadvantaged regions were closing at alarming rates as AI-driven platforms undercut traditional education costs. A Pew Research survey found that 25% of U.S. teachers believed AI tools like ChatGPT caused more harm than good in K-12 education. (Pew Research, 2024)

For students in affluent areas, AI-enhanced curriculums expanded their knowledge faster than ever. For the rest, education became an impersonal, algorithmic process—soulless, rigid, and designed to funnel them into a world where their futures had already been decided.

"The future of education is AI-driven," Pew Research noted. "But it is not equal." (Pew Research, 2026)

**Economic Inequality: A New Class of Untouchables**
AI-driven productivity boosted global GDP by 15%—but 95% of those gains flowed to the top 0.1% of income earners. (McKinsey, 2024)

The old middle class—those who had adapted, re-skilled, and survived the first wave of AI—now found themselves priced out of the new economy. Those who could afford AI augmentation—neural implants, cognitive enhancements, biotech advantages—thrived.

Those who couldn't? They weren't just unemployed. They were obsolete.

"AI-driven wealth creation is the most concentrated in modern history," the Center for Global Development noted. "The wealth divide is now widening exponentially." (Center for Global Development, 2024)

Work had become a privilege, not a right.
The new ruling class wasn't made up of politicians or business leaders. It was the technologists, the engineers, the algorithm architects—the ones who had built the very systems now dictating reality. Soon, they were no longer just engineers.

They were the Empire of the Elites—a class that did not rule through elections, laws, or force—but through the silent, unseen power of code.

**The Volcanic Eruption**
The volcanic eruptions of AI expansion were not followed by renewal.
There was no rebuilding—only a world where the few dictated the future, while the many struggled to survive it.

## ***Stage 3: Disruption of Ecosystems - AI Expansion (micro view)***

*The buzz of fluorescent lights hummed above as Mia Alvarez stood at the factory floor's edge, clipboard in hand. The room was massive, the kind of industrial expanse that once pulsed with life--dozens of workers shouting above the machinery, their banter filling the air. Now it was quiet, save for the rhythmic whirring of automated arms assembling precision parts at speeds no human could match.*

*Mia glanced at the row of workers standing behind their new AI-assist stations. There were fewer than she remembered. The workforce had been slashed in half since Harmony Precision Tools adopted the new Scent Technologies automation system. Those who remained had been "re-skilled," a word HR had thrown around as if it could mend the loss of jobs, pride, and purpose.*

*Mia herself had been spared the layoffs, but just barely. Her role as a line supervisor had shifted into something less tangible--a mix of overseeing human workers and troubleshooting the machines that now outnumbered them.*

*She sighed, adjusting her safety goggles as she surveyed her team. The promise of re-skilling had sounded noble at first: the company would train its workers to operate alongside the AI, integrating human ingenuity with machine efficiency. In reality, the training had been rushed, barely scratching the surface of what they needed to know.*

*Mia thought of Alberto, her closest friend on the floor, who'd been let go last month. He had been too slow to adapt to the new system, and when the machine-learning interface flagged his performance as "inefficient," there was no second chance.*

*Her clipboard trembled slightly in her grip as she remembered how he'd said goodbye: "We're just waiting for the machines to learn our jobs faster than we can."*

*A sharp beep jolted her back to the present. One of the machines had stalled, a robotic arm frozen mid-air. Before Mia could react, a green light blinked on her augmented reality glasses, overlaying diagnostic instructions in her field of vision. She tapped the interface on her wrist, initiating the repair process.*

*The glasses were part of the company's AI-assist system, touted as the key to keeping workers relevant. The headset delivered precise instructions directly to her vision, guiding her through tasks she once could have done blindfolded. Now, she relied on the AI to think for her, to tell her what buttons to press and what tools to use.*

*At first, she'd been grateful for the glasses. They had saved her job. But over time, she realized they had also taken something from her. The intuitive knowledge she'd spent years building was fading, replaced by dependence on the machine's cold, calculating precision.*

*"Mia," a voice called from across the floor. It was Jason, one of the younger workers who had taken to the AI systems like a fish to water. He was smiling, but his expression carried an edge of uncertainty. "The system flagged me for recalibration training again. Do you know if that's serious?"*

*Mia frowned. "Probably just means your numbers are dipping. They'll have you sit with HR, run you through the training again."*

*Jason nodded, but his smile faltered. They both knew what "recalibration" really meant: one step closer to the chopping block. The machines didn't care how hard you tried, how long you'd been with the company, or how much you needed the paycheck. They only cared about efficiency.*

*As Jason walked away, Mia felt the familiar knot tighten in her stomach. She couldn't reassure him, couldn't promise that things would get better. Because deep down, she didn't believe they would.*

*Later that night, Mia sat in her cramped apartment, the flickering light of her television casting long shadows across the room. The news anchor's voice droned on about the latest wave of AI-driven layoffs across the state. Another 10,000 jobs gone, another town struggling to adapt.*

*She turned the volume down, her gaze falling to the AR glasses sitting on her coffee table. The device that had saved her job was also slowly stripping her of her identity. She was no longer a skilled supervisor, no longer someone whose experience and intuition mattered. She was just an extension of the machine, following its instructions, meeting its demands.*

*Her phone buzzed. A message from her sister, asking if she could send money to help with their mother's medical bills. Mia stared at the screen for a long moment before setting the phone down. She didn't have the heart to tell her sister she wasn't sure how much longer she'd even have a paycheck.*

*The asteroid hadn't killed everything immediately. It had begun with a few clouds of dust, creeping over the horizon, spreading slowly until it blotted out the sky. For Mia Alvarez, those clouds were already here, choking the light, leaving her to wonder how long she could keep breathing.*

# CHAPTER 7

**L**ucas Bennett adjusted his tie as he stepped into the executive conference room. The space was sleek and minimalist, dominated by a single long table and a wall-length screen displaying live metrics from Harmony Falls. At the head of the table sat Nolan Scent, scrolling through data on a tablet. He didn't look up as Lucas entered, but the subtle tilt of his head signaled he'd noticed.

"Lucas," Nolan said without preamble, his voice as precise as the graphs on the screen. "What do you have for me?"

Lucas cleared his throat, feeling the weight of Nolan's attention even before he looked up. "Updates from Delta Precision Manufacturing, sir. And broader data points on Harmony Falls. I think you'll find the numbers... illuminating."

Nolan gestured toward the chair opposite him, his expression neutral. "Go ahead."

Lucas slid his tablet onto the table and swiped it to project his dashboard onto the wall screen. The room filled with the glow of cascading charts and figures.

"This is Delta Precision," Lucas began, pointing to the upward-trending graphs. "Since the full neural chip rollout six months ago, production efficiency has increased by 40%. Error margins are down to 0.02%, and absenteeism is virtually nonexistent. Revenue is up 35% year-over-year, and profits are projected to double within eighteen months."

Nolan studied the graphs, his face impassive. "And the workers?"

Lucas tapped the screen, pulling up another set of data. Worker Satisfaction Metrics. Smiling faces appeared, alongside words like *Fulfilled*, *Engaged*, and *Harmonious*. "Reported satisfaction rates are at an all-time high. Feedback surveys--filtered through the chip's sentiment analysis--show overwhelming positivity. Employees are not just performing well; they're thriving."

Nolan's lips curved into a faint smile. "Impressive."

Lucas hesitated for a fraction of a second before swiping to a confidential dashboard marked Compliance Metrics. The graphs here mirrored the previous ones, but their labels revealed the underlying mechanics: Desire Suppression, Ambition Modulation, Compliance Index.

"These metrics," Lucas said carefully, "show the other side of the equation. The neural chips aren't just enhancing productivity. They're recalibrating expectations. Dissatisfaction levels have been reduced by over 90%, and ambition beyond assigned roles has been effectively neutralized."

Nolan leaned forward, his attention sharp. "And it's working? No anomalies?"

Lucas hesitated, knowing this was the part Nolan would scrutinize most. "There are no significant anomalies. However..." He paused, tapping the screen to highlight a small cluster of flagged cases. "In a few instances, we've seen minor resistance. Typically, among workers who were previously outspoken or resistant to change. The chip adjusts over time, but we're monitoring closely."

Nolan's gaze lingered on the flagged cases for a moment before he leaned back in his chair. "You'll resolve them."

It wasn't a question, but Lucas nodded anyway. "Yes, sir."

Lucas swiped back to a broader dashboard showing Harmony Falls as a whole. "Delta Precision has become the cornerstone of Harmony Falls' success. The factory's metrics are unmatched, and its performance is driving economic stability in the town. In contrast, non-Nolan-owned businesses--like Harmony Freight--are struggling. Layoffs, bankruptcies, declining morale. They're barely hanging on."

Nolan's expression didn't change, but Lucas caught the glint of satisfaction in his eyes. "And the community impact?"

Lucas brought up another screen, this one showing qualitative data. "Community metrics are improving. Infrastructure spending is up, local businesses are benefiting, and social cohesion has increased by 27% since Delta began dominating the local economy."

Nolan raised an eyebrow. "Social cohesion?"

Lucas responded with certainty. "It's a sanitized term, sir. It means people are falling in line. They're accepting their roles, their places in the system. And for those in Delta, they're genuinely satisfied."

Nolan steepled his fingers, his gaze fixed on Lucas. "And Harmony Freight? How long until they collapse?"

"Two, maybe three months," Lucas replied. "They're hemorrhaging cash, and worker unrest is at a tipping point. Without intervention, they'll fold before the year is out."

"Good," Nolan said, his tone cool. "We'll offer them the neural chips as a lifeline. For free. The public will see it as a gesture of goodwill, and we'll prove that our system isn't just the future--it's the only future."

Lucas felt a swell of pride. "Understood, sir. The plan is progressing perfectly."

Nolan leaned back, his eyes gleaming. "This isn't just about Harmony Falls, Lucas. It's about redefining society. A new order. And we're the architects."

Lucas nodded firmly. As he left the room, he felt no hesitation, no second thoughts. He was Nolan's right hand, a part of the grand design that would shape humanity's future. Harmony Falls was the beginning, and Lucas knew he was exactly where he was meant to be: at the center of it all.

*The asteroid hadn't obliterated life on Earth in an instant. It had reshaped the conditions of survival, slowly, imperceptibly, until adaptation was no longer possible. Harmony Falls was no different. And as Lucas walked away, the weight of what he had built settled heavily on his shoulders.*

##

The Oval Office was steeped in tension, the kind that made the air feel heavier, oppressive. The President sat behind the Resolute Desk, his shoulders squared, his expression hardened by weeks of relentless crises. His senior advisors flanked him, their faces lined with exhaustion as they murmured about plummeting markets, escalating protests, and the looming specter of political collapse.

Nolan Scent stood across from them, perfectly at ease. His posture was relaxed, his expression calm—too calm, as though the chaos roiling outside the White House had nothing to do with him. It was infuriating.

The President leaned forward, his knuckles pressing against the desk. "Mr. Scent," he began, his voice sharp, "you've unleashed hell on this country. Entire industries are crumbling. Families are being destroyed. Cities are burning. And you're standing there as if none of this is your fault?"

Nolan said nothing, his calm silence only fueling the President's anger.

"You think you can shrug this off?" the President snapped, his voice rising. "You think your AI empire can run unchecked while millions of Americans are left with nothing? Not on my watch."

He gestured to an aide, who stepped forward and placed a thick folder on the desk. "Here's what's going to happen. Effective immediately, we're introducing legislation to halt AI advancements. Any company profiting from AI optimization without protecting jobs will face tariffs so steep it'll be cheaper to produce goods by hand. And you? You're going to face the kind of scrutiny that makes tax evasion charges look like parking tickets."

The President leaned back, waiting for Nolan to flinch, to protest. But Nolan didn't even blink.

"Is that all, Mr. President?" Nolan asked, his voice calm, his hands loosely clasped behind his back.

The President scowled. "That's all for now. But make no mistake—your empire is about to collapse."

Nolan stepped forward, his voice measured. "Mr. President, I have no intention of battling the United States government. Quite the opposite—I want to save it."

The President narrowed his eyes, caught off guard. "Save it? From what? You?"

"From collapse," Nolan said smoothly. "From the very chaos you just described. You can legislate, you can audit, you can impose tariffs—but you can't halt progress. At best, you can slow it down. And even if you did, it wouldn't solve the fundamental problem."

The President's glare hardened. "Which is?"

Nolan took his time, letting the question hang before answering. "Too many people. Too few resources. It's unsustainable. We've known this for decades; we've just been too afraid to admit it. The system you're trying to protect—it's already broken."

One of the advisors bristled. "And you think AI is the answer?"

Nolan smiled faintly, almost indulgently. "AI isn't the problem. It's the tool. What matters is how you use it. And right now, Mr. President, you're trying to fight a flood with sandbags."

Reaching into his pocket, Nolan produced a slim tablet and handed it across the desk. "This is Harmony Falls," he said. "A mid-sized town representing the challenges your administration is facing across the country."

The President glanced at the screen, scrolling through live metrics: productivity figures, economic activity, and worker satisfaction rates from Nolan-owned companies and their non-Nolan counterparts. Both sectors were struggling, but the contrast was stark. The Nolan businesses were holding steady, while the independents were spiraling toward collapse.

"These numbers don't look great for your companies either," the President noted, his tone skeptical.

"They don't," Nolan agreed, unfazed. "Not yet. I'm letting the system run its course. Because a quick fix won't solve this crisis—it'll only mask it. I need four weeks, Mr. President. Four weeks to show you that Harmony Falls isn't just a symptom of this chaos. It's the solution'"

The President studied Nolan, his suspicion unmasked. "And what's in it for you?"

Nolan's expression turned enigmatic. "Let me show you what can really be achieved. Then I'll tell you what I want."

#

The President sat in the now-empty Oval Office, his hand resting on a tumbler of whiskey he hadn't yet sipped. The room was heavy with silence, save for the faint hum of activity outside its doors. He stared at the Resolute Desk, the papers stacked neatly on its surface looking more like artefacts of a bygone era than tools of governance.

His Chief of Staff entered quietly, carrying a fresh folder of reports. "That man has the composure of a stone statue and the ambition of a Roman emperor," he remarked, breaking the stillness.

The President let out a low chuckle, though there was little humor in it. "And like any emperor worth his salt, he knows how to keep his empire intact."

"You think he'll deliver?" The Chief of Staff set the reports down and poured himself a glass from the decanter.

The President finally took a sip of his own drink, savoring the burn before responding. "I don't think he'll deliver anything that doesn't serve him first. But here's the thing about people like Nolan Scent--they will do absolutely everything to protect their money, their power. They'll burn the world to the ground before they let their empires fall."

The Chief of Staff arched an eyebrow. "Doesn't exactly inspire confidence, sir."

The President leaned back in his chair, his gaze hardening. "That's why he'll deliver. Because what's happening out there--the protests, the collapses, the disarray--it's a threat to everything men like him stand for. If anyone's going to find a way to stabilize the system, it's the guy who needs that system to keep printing him money."

He swirled his glass, the amber liquid catching the light. "The thing about the elites is they always find a way to survive. And I wouldn't trust anyone else to be as motivated as Nolan Scent to make sure this thing doesn't come crashing down on their heads."

The Chief of Staff nodded slowly, his skepticism giving way to reluctant agreement. "So, you're betting that his self-interest is the key?"

The President drained the last of his whiskey and set the glass down with a deliberate finality. "I'm not betting, John. I'm hedging. And if Nolan Scent wants to save his empire, I'll make damn sure he saves the country in the process."

The Chief of Staff stood silently for a moment, then picked up the untouched reports. "We've got to hope your hedge pays off, sir. Because if it doesn't..."

The President's voice cut through, resolute. "It will. Men like Scent don't lose. Not when their own survival is on the line."

He rose from his chair, the weight of his words echoing in the room as he stared out the window at the sprawling city beyond. "And if he does manage to fix this, maybe the rest of us will have a shot at survival too."

##

# CHAPTER 8

The lab thrummed with quiet purpose, its air thick with sterile precision. Monitors blinked in rhythm, and the faint whir of Milo's support systems created a hypnotic backdrop. Ethan Numan stood at his workstation, eyes flicking between the display and Milo's motionless form. A deep crease lined his brow, his focus unbroken until Nolan Scent entered the room.

"Ethan." Nolan's tone was conversational, as if he were walking into a casual meeting rather than one of the most advanced laboratories in existence. "How's Milo today?"

Ethan turned, his face composed but tired. "The same as yesterday. Stable, compliant. Progress is... steady."

Nolan tilted his head, a faint smile curling at the edges of his lips. "Steady. That doesn't sound like the breakthrough pace you're known for."

Ethan exhaled sharply, gesturing toward Milo's setup. "This isn't a sprint, Nolan. Neural mapping isn't just data collection. It's recreating the essence of consciousness itself. And Milo's condition makes this both an unprecedented opportunity and an impossible challenge."

Nolan stepped closer, his eyes scanning the room, lingering briefly on Milo's still form. "So, what's the latest?"

Ethan adjusted his stance, his voice measured. "We've refined the neural maps to about 70% accuracy, but the remaining 30% is unpredictable—human consciousness isn't a machine. Every synaptic connection, every anomaly, matters. And without additional test subjects..." He trailed off, shaking his head. "It's years away from being replicable. Milo's condition is unique, and we only have one quantum system capable of this level of computation. That's a bottleneck no one else in the world is dealing with."

"How many years?" Nolan's question was deceptively casual.

Ethan hesitated. "Five. Maybe more."

"Five?" Nolan repeated, his tone soft but sharp.

Ethan straightened, meeting Nolan's gaze. "This isn't a matter of brute force, Nolan. It's about understanding. Pushing faster doesn't just risk failure—it risks losing Milo."

Nolan began pacing slowly, his hands clasped behind his back. His voice dropped an octave, thoughtful yet persistent. "What if none of that mattered?"

Ethan frowned. "What are you talking about?"

"What if you didn't have bottlenecks?" Nolan said, stopping mid-step. "No regulatory hurdles. No ethical debates. Unlimited compute power, unlimited resources. Test subjects at your disposal. What then?"

Ethan blinked, his jaw tightening. "That's not how this works, Nolan. Those aren't obstacles—they're the framework. Take them away, and it's not science anymore. It's chaos."

"Is it?" Nolan countered, his voice smooth. "Think. If you had none of those constraints—if you could do whatever was necessary without limits—how far could you take this? How quickly?"

The silence in the lab was almost deafening. Ethan ran a hand through his hair, his expression torn between disbelief and frustration. "Even if I entertain that—hypothetically—what you're asking for is impossible. This isn't a race. There are no shortcuts."

"Humor me," Nolan pressed. "Let's say it wasn't impossible. Let's say you had everything."

Ethan finally sighed, rubbing his temples. "If there were no constraints? If I could do everything I wanted, when I wanted? Then... maybe two years. But that's absurd. The obstacles are real. Milo's condition alone makes this a minefield of uncertainty."

"And if the obstacles weren't real?" Nolan's tone was calm, but his words carried an almost imperceptible weight.

Ethan froze, staring at Nolan. For a brief moment, something unspoken passed between them. Finally, Ethan said, "If you're asking me to imagine a world without rules, I can't. Because if that's

the world you're envisioning, it's not one I want to be a part of."
Nolan smiled faintly, stepping toward the door. "You're a good man, Ethan. Stay focused on Milo. Let me worry about the rest."
With that, he left, the quiet hum of the lab resuming as Ethan stood motionless, a cold knot settling in his chest.

#

Molly sat perched on the edge of her chair, her composed expression carrying a hint of intensity. The sunlight filtering through the tall windows of Nolan's office caught the sharp glint in her bracelet as she turned it absently around her wrist.

"How's it going with Jansen?" Nolan's voice was calm, but his gaze was intent.
Molly's pause was measured, her response deliberate. "He's... compelling. Frustratingly so. He's not extreme, not a crackpot. He's deliberate, methodical, and he asks the kind of questions that stick."
Nolan leaned back slightly, his expression neutral but attentive.
"He's raising doubts," she continued. "Not just in others--in me too, if I'm honest. He talks about purpose and what we're really building toward. He's careful, precise. It makes him... dangerous." Her lips pressed into a thin line. "I see why people listen to him."
Nolan's lips curved into a faint smile. "So, you think he's a problem."
Molly met his gaze evenly. "Yes. He's voicing the concerns of the country, and he's good at it. Better than most. If he keeps this up, the narrative we've built could start to fray."
Nolan regarded her silently for a moment before leaning forward, his tone steady and deliberate. "Stay close to him, Molly. Let him talk. Let him ask his questions, air his doubts. Don't argue with him. Just listen."
Molly nodded slowly, absorbing his instructions with a keen edge of understanding. "And then?"
"Get him to Harmony Falls," Nolan said simply.

She tilted her head slightly. "Harmony Falls will be enough to derail him?" There was no naivety in her tone, only a calculated curiosity.
"I don't need him derailed." Nolan's faint smile returned, cold and certain. "I need him to see. To talk himself out of credibility in the face of what we've built."
Molly's lips curved slightly, a touch of her father's own steel in her expression. "And if that doesn't work?"
Nolan studied her for a long moment, then leaned back in his chair, his voice calm but resolute. "Then we'll have to show him," he said, his tone carrying finality. "And make sure everyone else sees the truth."
Molly held his gaze for a moment, then said with quiet confidence, "I've already invited him to Harmony Falls."
Nolan's eyes flickered with a hint of surprise before a pleased smile spread across his face. "Good," he said, his voice approving. "Very good."
Molly nodded with cool composure, the weight of their shared strategy evident as she rose to leave.

#

Lucas Bennett adjusted his tie as he approached Nolan's office. It wasn't like Nolan to summon him twice in such quick succession on the same topic, especially after they'd already gone over the Harmony Falls metrics in detail earlier. Something had shifted, and Lucas suspected it had to do with the President.

He pushed open the heavy door and stepped inside. The air felt colder, the space somehow more foreboding than usual. Nolan sat at his desk, the glow of his tablet reflecting off his sharp features. He didn't look up as Lucas entered, but his voice was as precise as ever.
"The chips," Nolan said without preamble, his tone clipped. "It's time."
Lucas hesitated for the briefest moment, then stepped further into

the room. "You want the control mechanisms activated."

Nolan nodded, his gaze unrelenting. "Quietly. No announcements, no warnings. Seamless."

Lucas tilted his head slightly, his mind already calculating. "And the metrics?"

"The performance metrics will be the public-facing story," Nolan replied, rising from his chair and pacing to the floor-to-ceiling windows. "Efficiency, productivity, satisfaction levels--all glowing. That's what the President and the public will see."

"And the compliance metrics?" Lucas asked, his voice lower.

"They're for us," Nolan said without hesitation, turning to face Lucas. "Not for the President. Not for the regulators. Not for anyone outside this room."

Lucas's lips curved into a faint smirk. "Understood."

Nolan's gaze sharpened. "The President is applying pressure. He needs results--fast. Harmony Falls has to be airtight. Every loose end tied up, every potential problem handled before his return."

Lucas nodded thoughtfully. "And Jansen?"

Nolan's expression darkened, his tone sharper now. "He's dangerous. If he spins this as manipulation or control, it could derail everything."

Lucas leaned forward slightly, his demeanor calm but calculating. "We need a tangible way to neutralize him. Something tied to his own rhetoric--his so-called empathy for people. Turn his strength into his weakness."

Nolan arched an eyebrow. "I'm listening."

Lucas tapped his fingers on the edge of the table. "A family. A case that tugs at the heartstrings but showcases the power of the chips. Something undeniable. If we can find the right family--one desperate for help, with everything to gain from our technology--it'll be a public relations masterpiece."

"And it affects Jansen how?" Nolan pressed, his tone clipped.

Lucas smirked faintly, his confidence unwavering. "We let him believe the family has reservations about the chips. He'll see it as an opportunity to 'save' them, to prove himself right. But when the family embraces the technology instead--and does so publicly--it'll destroy his credibility. He'll look like a self-righteous meddler who's out of touch with reality."

Nolan leaned back in his chair, considering the plan. "And you're confident this will work?"

Lucas nodded. "I'll need to identify the right family. Someone local to Harmony Falls. We use our connections--doctors, community contacts--to pinpoint a case that fits perfectly. From there, the narrative builds itself."

Nolan's gaze lingered on Lucas for a long moment before he gave a sharp nod. "Do it. Quietly. And make sure the story spreads far and wide when it happens."

Lucas rose, his posture straight and assured. "Consider it done."

As he turned to leave, Nolan's voice stopped him. "And Lucas, don't let the execution slip. This has to be perfect."

Lucas glanced back, a faint smirk tugging at the corner of his lips. "I understand, sir. Jansen won't know what hit him."

"And Molly? Do you want her to know about the control mechanisms?"

Nolan paused, his eyes narrowing slightly. "Not yet," he said evenly, his tone measured. "Her time will come."

Nolan turned back to the window, his voice quieter but no less resolute. "The President wants results, Lucas. And I'm going to give him a solution so complete he won't dare question it. We move now--fast and flawless."

Lucas nodded, leaving the room with purpose. Whatever urgency Nolan had felt from the President's demands, it was now squarely on his shoulders.

Nolan stood alone, staring at the skyline. Harmony Falls would be the showcase, the proof of concept--and the President's visit would cement it all. Nothing could be left to chance.

##

# CHAPTER 9

**On**e week later a private jet descended smoothly onto the airstrip near Harmony Falls, the hum of its engines fading as it taxied to a halt. Molly glanced out the window at the modest terminal, a stark contrast to the bustling, tech-driven world of the Bay Area. The transition felt like stepping into another reality.

She adjusted her bracelet absently as the cabin door opened, the sharp air of America's heartland rushing in. A sleek, black Scent Technologies car was already waiting at the base of the stairs, its AI systems purring softly as they approached.

Jansen followed Molly down the steps, his gaze scanning the quiet surroundings. "The juxtaposition is striking," he remarked. "Tech-bro opulence meets small-town simplicity."

Molly gave a small smile, but her mind was elsewhere. "Harmony Falls isn't simple," she replied. "It's a prototype. My father would call it a proof of concept."

They slid into the plush car seats, and the AI seamlessly took over, guiding the vehicle toward the town center. Molly stared out the window as farmland gave way to tidy streets and clusters of buildings, the silence between them broken only by the occasional hum of the car's systems.

Jansen reached into his bag, pulling out a compact leather case. "We've got time," he said, setting a backgammon board on the retractable table between them. "Fancy a game?"

Molly arched an eyebrow. "You carry a backgammon set everywhere?"

Jansen smirked as he arranged the pieces. "Old habits die hard. Helps me think."

Molly leaned forward, curious despite herself. "I haven't played in years, but fine. Let's see what you've got."

The dice clicked softly as Jansen tossed them, and the game began.

Molly played with her usual determination, but no matter how carefully she strategized, Jansen outmanoeuvred her at every turn.

"You're annoyingly good at this," she muttered, watching him make yet another calculated move.

"It's not about being good," Jansen replied. "Backgammon is a mix of strategy, chance, and adaptability. You can't control the dice, but you can control how you respond to them."

Molly frowned, moving her piece. "And if the dice always roll against you?"

Jansen leaned back, smiling faintly. "Then you learn to make even the worst rolls work in your favor."

As they approached the outskirts of Harmony Falls, Jansen's tone grew softer. "Do you ever think about your mother?"

The question caught Molly off guard. She paused mid-move, her expression tightening. "Why?"

"Because," Jansen said carefully, "it's a near-death experience of sorts. Life and death, colliding in a moment. You survived. She didn't."

Molly's face hardened. "It's not something I dwell on. Her death was a complication—random, meaningless."

"Do you believe that?" Jansen asked, studying her.

Molly shrugged, her voice clipped. "Some people get lucky. Some don't. If you're about to turn this into a cosmic lecture on fate, don't bother."

Jansen didn't press further, though his gaze lingered on her for a moment. "Not fate," he said quietly. "But maybe not nothing, either. Collisions like that... they leave marks. Even if we don't want them to."

Molly turned back to the window, her expression unreadable. The quiet tension between them filled the car as Harmony Falls came into view, its clean streets and orderly rows of buildings basking in the afternoon sun.

"Another game?" Jansen asked lightly, attempting to break the silence.

Molly smirked faintly, shaking her head. "Not now. But next time, you're going down."

The car's AI announced their arrival as it slowed to a stop near the town center. Molly exhaled, her gaze fixed on the carefully crafted façade of Harmony Falls. Whatever came next, it would require more than strategy or luck to win.

The Scent car entered Harmony Falls with an effortless glide, its sleek frame standing out against the unassuming backdrop of the town. Molly glanced out the window, her expression neutral, but her eyes absorbed every detail of the scene. Jansen, seated beside her, shifted slightly in his seat, his gaze following hers.

The main street stretched ahead, lined with buildings that had seen better days. A faded mural on the side of a hardware store depicted a cheerful, bygone era—farmers, factory workers, and families smiling in front of neat homes. The paint had cracked and peeled, giving the faces an unsettling, ghostly quality.

A cluster of storefronts came into view. Some still had "For Lease" signs taped crookedly in their windows, while others were boarded up entirely. The few shops that remained open displayed handwritten sales signs in the hopes of drawing in dwindling foot traffic. A lone boutique boasted a "50% Closing Down Sale" banner, its bold red letters a sharp contrast to the faded awning above.

On the corner, a once-busy diner now stood quiet. The neon "Open" sign flickered erratically, the hum of its light barely audible as they passed. Through the windows, a waitress leaned against the counter, her face turned toward the door in a quiet vigil for customers who might not come.

"It's quieter than I expected," Molly said, her voice carefully composed.

Jansen glanced at her, his eyes thoughtful. "Quieter's one word for it."

Further down the street, they passed a small park. The grass had grown patchy in places, with weeds creeping through the cracks in the sidewalk. The playground equipment, once vibrant with color, had faded to dull shades of blue and red. A single child sat on a swing, idly kicking the dirt beneath her feet, her movements listless. A man—her father, perhaps—sat on a nearby bench, staring at his phone with a blank expression.

The Scent car slowed as they approached a modest factory on the outskirts of town. Unlike the businesses on Main Street, this building hummed with activity. Workers streamed out for a shift change, their uniforms crisp, their expressions placid. The parking lot was clean and orderly, every space occupied.

"Delta Precision Manufacturing," Molly said, reading the sign as the car turned into the driveway. "This is one of ours."

Jansen's gaze shifted toward the workers. "They don't seem worried about their jobs."

Molly smiled faintly. "Why would they be? They're part of something efficient, something stable. That's the future."

Jansen didn't respond immediately, his focus lingering on the workers as they walked to their cars. Their movements were calm, almost unnervingly so, as if the hum of the factory had settled into their very beings. He glanced back at the town they'd passed, the quiet streets and faded buildings a stark contrast to the efficiency before him.

"Interesting future," he said finally, his tone unreadable.

The car came to a stop at the entrance, where Lucas Bennett stood waiting, his posture confident and his smile welcoming. Molly stepped out of the car, smoothing her jacket, ready to begin the next stage of their visit.

#

The conference room was sleek and modern, dominated by a wide screen glowing with a meticulously prepared presentation. Lucas Bennett stood at the head of the table, his posture confident, his expression animated. Molly sat to his right, her tablet open in front of her, while Jansen leaned back in his chair, arms crossed, observing with a quiet intensity.

"Thank you both for making the time to visit," Lucas began, his voice warm, almost theatrical. "I know the drive through town must've been... sobering. Harmony Falls is in transition, no doubt about it. But transitions are painful by nature, and we're on the cusp of something extraordinary."

With a flick of his hand, the screen shifted to display trend-lines, bar graphs, and pie charts. The data was pristine, the visuals sharp and optimistic.

"This," Lucas said, pointing to a chart showing worker satisfaction levels, "is what's happening inside our companies. Productivity is up by 18%, absenteeism is down by 32%, and employee satisfaction scores--measured through anonymous feedback, of course--are the highest we've ever seen."

He clicked to another slide, showing a heat map of economic recovery in Harmony Falls. "And here's how it's affecting the community. Businesses near our operations--grocers, gas stations, local services--are reporting increased revenue. Stability inside the factories ripples outwards. This is what progress looks like."

Molly nodded, impressed by the clarity of the data. "It's hard to argue with the numbers."

Jansen remained silent, his eyes fixed on the screen. Lucas continued, undeterred.

"Here's the thing," Lucas said, pacing slightly. "We're not just fixing problems--we're proving that good business and happy people aren't mutually exclusive. We've cracked the code. This is scalable, sustainable progress. Harmony Falls isn't just a town. It's a model."

The presentation ended with a flourish, and Lucas turned to face them, clearly expecting praise. Molly leaned forward, her enthusiasm evident. "This is incredible, Lucas. The data speaks for itself."

Jansen's silence stretched for a beat too long, drawing their attention. Finally, he spoke, his tone measured. "It is impressive.

The metrics, the results--it's hard to argue with success."
Lucas smiled, smugly satisfied.
"But," Jansen continued, his gaze steady, "I wonder how much of this is necessary. Is progress for its own sake worth the cost? At what point do we stop and ask if this is the right way forward?"
Lucas's smile faltered, then morphed into something mocking. "Professor, with respect, if your dinosaurs were smarter, maybe they'd have invented a big net to catch the meteor. Or a fan powerful enough to blow away the clouds that blotted out the sun. But no, they just carried on doing not a lot as they went extinct."
Jansen's face remained calm, but there was a flicker of something darker in his eyes. He stood slowly, adjusting his jacket as he made his way toward the door.
Lucas raised an eyebrow. "No rebuttal? That's not like you."
Jansen stopped at the threshold and turned, his voice cool and deliberate. "You're right, Lucas. The dinosaurs didn't do a lot. They carried on for about 165 million years before a falling rock got the better of them."
He paused, letting the weight of his words sink in. "Humanity won't need a rock. We'll do it to ourselves in a fraction of the time. About a hundred thousand years, or less than one percent of the time the dinosaurs ruled the Earth."
For a moment, the room was silent. Molly looked down, avoiding Jansen's gaze, while Lucas smirked faintly, unshaken.
Jansen lingered just long enough to let his words settle before stepping out, leaving behind a quiet tension that no data point could smooth over.

##

# CHAPTER 10

The diner was a quiet hum of activity, the kind of place where locals lingered over coffee and conversations flowed like a gentle current. Molly and Jansen sat in a booth near the window, their breakfasts half-eaten. Molly stirred her coffee absently, her eyes narrowing as she studied Jansen across the table.

"I don't get you," she said finally, breaking the comfortable silence.

Jansen raised an eyebrow, pausing mid-bite of his toast. "What's not to get?"

She leaned forward, her tone sharper than intended. "The data told a great story yesterday. It wasn't doom and gloom. It didn't scream end of times. It was positive—progress, stability, recovery. So why the big extinction rant?"

Jansen set his toast down carefully, brushing crumbs from his hands. "You think that was a rant?"

"Yes," Molly said firmly. "And it wasn't necessary. You didn't need to like Bennett to accept the truth of the data."

Jansen chuckled softly, the sound dry but not unkind. "Fair point."

Molly blinked, surprised by the easy concession. "That's it? No counterargument? No philosophical deep dive?"

Jansen leaned back in his seat, considering her for a moment. "Maybe I am the dinosaur," he said quietly, his gaze drifting out the window.

The diner door opened, and a gentle breeze swept through, carrying with it the faint scent of freshly cut grass. Jansen turned his head slightly, as if acknowledging the wind itself. He looked back at Molly, a wry smile tugging at his lips.

"But," he said, his tone shifting, "maybe Mr. Bennett didn't show us all the data."

Molly stiffened, her eyes narrowing. "What's that supposed to mean?"

Jansen raised his hands in mock surrender before she could launch into a defense. "OK, OK. I'll accept the good progress story if the data, the people—if it all aligns. Fair?"
Molly relaxed slightly, though her expression remained skeptical. "Fair."
The waitress approached their table, refilling their coffee without a word. As she walked away, Jansen tapped the edge of his cup thoughtfully.
"For what it's worth," he said, glancing at Molly, "I don't think you're part of some grand conspiracy."
Molly smirked faintly, rolling her eyes. "Glad to hear it."
"But," Jansen continued, his tone soft but insistent, "when you're trying to fix the world, sometimes it's hard to see when the solutions create new problems."
Molly didn't reply immediately, her eyes dropping to her coffee as the hum of the diner filled the silence.
"Eat your eggs, we have a full day ahead touring the facility," she said finally, her tone light but her expression distant.
Jansen chuckled again, picking up his toast. "Yes, ma'am."
Outside the diner, the breeze lingered, swirling leaves and dust in lazy spirals before fading into stillness.

#

The group strolled through the expansive Delta Precision Manufacturing campus, sunlight pouring through the factory's glass atrium. Workers moved about their tasks with calm purpose, a sense of quiet satisfaction in their expressions. The faint hum of advanced machinery provided a steady backdrop to Lucas Bennett's confident explanations.

Molly walked beside Lucas, nodding along as he pointed out the facility's innovations. Jansen followed slightly behind, his gaze drifting between the workers and the polished, almost serene environment around him.

"This is where the future begins," Lucas said, gesturing toward a line of workers overseeing the assembly of precision components. "AI handles the heavy lifting--optimization, quality control, logistics. But our people remain central to the process. They guide the technology, provide human oversight."

Jansen glanced at the line of workers. There were fewer than he'd expect for a factory of this size, but their demeanors caught his attention. They seemed... content. Not forced or robotic, but genuinely at ease, as though the stress and uncertainty of life outside the factory had been left at the door.

"You've streamlined the workforce," Jansen observed, his voice neutral. "Where are the others?"

Lucas didn't miss a beat. "Reallocated," he said smoothly. "Many are still with Delta Precision, but in roles that suit their strengths--cleaning, maintenance, support. Others have taken positions in the local economy, like postal services, farms, and logistics. Harmony Falls is evolving, Professor, and its people are evolving with it."

"And they're satisfied?" Jansen pressed, his tone sharp enough to draw Molly's attention.

Lucas smiled, his confidence unwavering. "Absolutely. Our neural chips have been instrumental in helping people adjust to their new roles. It's a win-win--they're less stressed, more focused, and genuinely content with their contributions."

Molly jumped in, her voice enthusiastic. "And that's the goal, isn't it? To create a system where people can thrive, where they can find fulfilment no matter what they're doing?"

Jansen turned his gaze to her, noting the conviction in her voice. "Fulfilment," he echoed, his tone unreadable.

The tour continued outside, where workers loaded goods onto waiting trucks. Nearby, a small group of postal employees sorted packages, their movements unhurried but purposeful. Across the road, a logistics hub hummed with activity, workers directing automated forklifts and drones as they moved goods in and out of sleek storage facilities. Everywhere Jansen looked, he saw people going about their tasks with a kind of contented simplicity.

Molly gestured toward the bustling activity. "Look at this," she said, her voice brimming with approval. "It's a town reborn. People working, businesses thriving, the economy stabilized. It's everything we've been working toward."

Jansen watched a group of farmhands talking and laughing as they loaded crates of vegetables onto a truck. They looked genuinely happy, their smiles easy and natural. He couldn't deny the scene's surface appeal, but something about it unsettled him.

"And this contentment," he said, turning to Lucas. "It's because of the chips?"

Lucas met his gaze evenly. "The chips help, sure. They reduce stress, improve focus, and allow people to embrace their roles with clarity. But it's more than that. It's a community that works."

Jansen didn't respond immediately, his eyes returning to the workers. He saw no signs of dissatisfaction, no tension or frustration. It all seemed so... natural. Too natural.

Molly broke the silence, her tone light but probing. "What do you think, Professor? Isn't this what progress should look like?"

Jansen turned to her, his expression contemplative. "It's remarkable," he admitted. "But progress always comes with a cost. The question is who pays it."

Lucas's smile widened. "That's the beauty of this system--no one has to pay. It's harmony, Professor. Pure and simple, pun intended."

Jansen said nothing, his gaze lingering on the scene before him. The idyllic picture Lucas painted was flawless on the surface, but beneath it, he felt an intangible sense of unease. The people of Harmony Falls were happy, no doubt--but at what price?

The tour of Delta Precision Manufacturing had concluded, and Lucas Bennett was basking in Molly's praise as they walked back toward the main office. Jansen, however, had grown quiet, his eyes distant as if his thoughts were elsewhere.

"Excuse me for a moment," Jansen said suddenly, stopping at the edge of the parking lot. "I need some air. Maybe stretch my legs."

Molly glanced at him, mildly surprised. "We're almost done, Professor. I'm sure Lucas can answer any lingering questions."

Jansen gave her a faint smile. "I'm not much for corporate wrap-ups. I'll meet you back here in a bit."

Bennett shrugged, clearly unbothered. "Take your time. Harmony Falls is a friendly place."

Jansen nodded and turned toward the park they had passed when driving in with Molly. It had caught his attention then, a small green space in a town overshadowed by its industrial past. Now, as he approached, he noticed the quiet wear of the place--the faded paint on the playground, the cracks in the benches, the weeds poking through the edges of the paths. It was a reflection of the broader struggle he had seen in the town. He lingered near a rusted water fountain, observing a small gathering of people seated on a bench nearby.

Jansen approached casually, offering a polite nod. "Mind if I sit?"

The group glanced at him, wary but not hostile. The man in flannel shrugged. "Suit yourself."

Jansen sat down, taking a moment to gauge their mood. "It's a quiet town," he said, gesturing around. "Different from what I expected."

The woman with the stroller scoffed. "Quiet's one way to put it. Dead is another."

Jansen raised an eyebrow. "Dead?"

She sighed, her voice edged with bitterness. "What's left? My husband got laid off six months ago. Factory work's all he's ever known, and now he's doing shifts at a farm just to keep us afloat. It's not enough, but at least it's something. Better than nothing, I guess."

"And your friends or family--how are they managing?" Jansen asked, keeping his tone neutral.

The younger man leaning against the tree chimed in, his voice tinged with resentment. "My brother's at Delta Precision. Same layoffs hit him, but he took one of those 'alternative positions.' Cleaning machines, fetching tools, whatever they tell him to do. Says he's fine with it--happy, even. Like he doesn't care that he used to

run the machines, not scrub them."
The man in flannel finally spoke, his voice low and gruff. "My wife's the same. She works for one of those Scent companies now. Used to hate her job, always complained about the long hours, the stress. Now she's doing data entry or something--part-time, no benefits--and she's... fine. Smiles when she talks about it. Says it's 'less pressure.'" He shook his head. "Doesn't make sense."
"Does it bother you?" Jansen asked, his question pointed but not accusatory.
Flannel hesitated, glancing at the others. "I mean, yeah. A little. I get wanting to make the best of things, but it's like she's a whole different person now. We used to talk about saving up, moving somewhere better. Now she doesn't even think about it. Says she's happy where we are."
The woman with the stroller nodded. "Same with my sister. Used to dream about starting her own business. Now she's delivering mail and says it's the best thing that's ever happened to her. It's like... like they're too comfortable being stuck."
The younger man leaned forward, his voice quieter now. "It's strange, right? Good for them, I guess. But I can't figure how they'd just stop wanting... more."
Jansen frowned slightly, absorbing their words. "And you think the chips have something to do with this?"
The group shifted uncomfortably. Flannel was the first to speak. "The chips? Nah. They're just supposed to help with focus or keep stress down. Tiny things like that couldn't change someone, right?"
Jansen leaned forward, his tone calm but deliberate. "Small things can have big effects. Think about aspirin--one tablet can stop pain, lower your fever. Or antidepressants, which can shift a person's whole outlook on life. It doesn't take much."
The group exchanged uneasy glances, their skepticism giving way to something closer to unease. The woman with the stroller shook her head slowly. "It's not like that. It's just work stress. They've been through a lot. Maybe they're just... adjusting."
Jansen nodded, not pressing further. But his thoughts churned as he

stood and brushed off his jacket. "Sometimes, when people go through tough changes, they find ways to cope--ways to make things seem better than they are. Maybe that's what's happening here."

The man in flannel snorted. "If that's coping, I'd like some of whatever they're drinking."

Jansen gave a thin smile. "It's not always about what you're drinking," he said quietly, "but who's pouring."

The group fell silent, exchanging uncertain glances as Jansen walked away, his mind racing. The contentment he'd seen at Delta Precision wasn't natural--it couldn't be. And if the chips could influence thoughts, even slightly, what else were they capable of?

It wasn't a conspiracy in the group's eyes--not yet. But to Jansen, it was becoming impossible to ignore the evidence. Something deeper was happening in Harmony Falls. And Nolan Scent was at the center of it.

##

# CHAPTER 11

The glass-walled meeting room overlooked the pristine rooftop garden of Scent Laboratories, the gentle rustle of leaves barely audible through the soundproof windows. Ethan Numan leaned back in his chair, his posture relaxed but his sharp eyes fixed on Dr. Meredith Park as she scrolled through a tablet.

"Overall, Project Heal's progress is steady," Park began, her tone brisk. "We've seen consistent improvements across all subject categories—motor function restoration, memory retrieval, emotional stability. The implant updates rolled out seamlessly."

Ethan nodded, tapping his pen absently against the table. "Milo's baseline activity continues to increase. No setbacks with the quantum integration, though it's still slow. But slow is better than catastrophic."

Park chuckled lightly. "I'll take 'slow but steady' over catastrophic any day." They shared a brief smile. Despite the high stakes of their work, there was a mutual respect that kept their interactions professional yet friendly. Park set her tablet down, folding her hands neatly. "Anything else on your end?"

Ethan hesitated. "Actually, there's something I wanted to ask you—off the record."

Park's brow furrowed slightly, but she nodded. "Of course."

Ethan's voice lowered. "I had a conversation with Nolan. He asked me a… hypothetical question. No restrictions. No limitations. No regulations. How quickly I could make progress."

Park's lips tightened. "And what did you tell him?"

"I tried to brush it off," Ethan admitted. "But he pressed. I gave him an estimate, reluctantly. And now I can't stop thinking about it. He's planning something, Meredith. Something bigger than he's letting on."

Park frowned. "He hasn't approached me with anything like that.

It's business as usual on my end—progress reports, updates, nothing out of the ordinary."

Ethan exhaled, a mix of relief and frustration. "Good. Let me know if that changes, though. I'm worried he might push us to paint way outside the lines."

"I will," Park said. "And for the record, I'm with you. We do this properly, or we don't do it at all."

Ethan nodded, reassured. "Thanks. That's all I needed to hear."

Park hesitated, biting her lip. "Actually… Ethan, there's something I've been meaning to tell you. Something I'm not sure what to make of."

Ethan raised an eyebrow. "What is it?"

She shifted in her seat. "We've been getting… odd readings from the Project Heal subjects."

"What kind of readings?"

Park held up a hand. "I know, I know. But it's hard to explain. In the past week, every single subject has registered as brain dead at some point. Briefly, but it's happened. And then their neural activity returns to normal as if nothing happened."

Ethan blinked. "Brain dead? That can't be. Are you sure?"

Park bristled slightly. "Ethan, this is my lab. My team. Some of the best neuroscientists on the planet. We triple-checked everything."

He rubbed the bridge of his nose. "That doesn't make any sense."

"No, it doesn't," Park agreed. "And I haven't seen any side effects—no behavioral changes, no cognitive degradation. But I can't explain why it's happening or if it'll happen again. And if it ever becomes permanent…"

"Have you seen anything like this with Milo?" she asked.

Ethan shook his head. "No. Nothing even close. But his setup is so different—quantum integration, unique hardware, custom coding. It's apples and oranges compared to Project Heal."

Park sighed. "I thought you might have some insight."

Ethan sat back. "This is… weird. Really weird. I'll stop by your lab when I can, look at the data myself. Maybe there's something you missed, or something I can see from a different angle."

Park's shoulders eased slightly. "I'd appreciate that. Thank you."

Ethan stood, a pensive look crossing his face. "If anything else happens, you let me know immediately. And Meredith, keep this between us for now. The last thing we need is Nolan catching wind of this."

Park nodded. "Agreed."

As Ethan walked away, his mind churned. Brain-dead readings? It didn't add up. And yet, the implications lingered like a shadow at the edge of his thoughts, dark and undefined.

##

# CHAPTER 12

The sun dipped lower in the sky, casting Harmony Falls in hues of gold and crimson as Molly checked her watch for the third time. She stood near the edge of the town square, her polished demeanor masking the unease that churned beneath the surface.

Jansen had just muttered something about needing time alone to "soak in the ambiance of decline" before wandering off toward the park they'd passed earlier.

Molly didn't stop him. In fact, she welcomed it.

Her phone buzzed in her hand, snapping her out of her thoughts. A calendar notification blinked on the screen:

*Rebecca Scent – Birthday.*

Molly's heart sank, the weight of the date hitting her like a physical blow. How had she forgotten? Every year, this day was etched into her family's unspoken calendar—a day of silence, of retreat. And of her father, locked away in that room, spiraling into the memories of the woman who had been the love of his life.

She hit a speed dial number. The voice of the head of staff, a composed older woman named Mrs. Briggs, answered on the second ring.

"Yes, Miss Scent?"

Molly spoke quickly, her voice tight. "Briggs, can you check something for me? Go to Dad's room and look at the bedside table. See if there's an open box there."

A pause. Then, muffled footsteps. Molly's stomach twisted as she waited, the seconds stretching into an eternity.

Finally, Briggs returned. "Yes, Miss Scent. There's an open box by the bedside table."

Molly closed her eyes. The necklace. The FG necklace.

He hadn't touched it in years—not since… that night.

She clenched her jaw and straightened her shoulders. "Thank you, Briggs. Please make sure no one disturbs him until I get back."

"Of course, Miss Scent. Is everything alright?"

"I'll be there soon."

She ended the call and turned, scanning the horizon for the Scent Technologies helicopter that was supposed to take her to the regional airport. As if on cue, the familiar thrum of rotors cut through the air. The sleek black chopper appeared over the rooftops, descending toward the helipad near the Nolan-owned factory.

Her heels clicked against the pavement as she strode toward it, her pace quickening. She climbed in without a word, nodding curtly to the pilot.

"Take me to the airport. Fast."

The pilot acknowledged her with a sharp nod, and within moments, the helicopter lifted off, its rotors slicing through the late afternoon sky. Molly settled into her seat, her mind already on the private jet waiting to whisk her to Silicon Valley.

She leaned back, staring out at the shifting landscape below. Her father's rare smile when he spoke of Rebecca. The way he'd once looked at Molly as if she were a miracle herself.

Those moments had grown fewer and further between, replaced by an intensity that sometimes felt like love and sometimes like an unbearable weight.

The sun dipped lower as they flew, the horizon shifting from gold to deep orange. Molly checked her watch again.

They'd be home soon.

#

The steady hum of the jet engines filled the cabin, a low vibration threading through the plush seat beneath her. Molly leaned her head against the cool window, watching as the clouds gave way to the patchwork of streets and fields below, blurring into a mosaic of muted greens and browns.

Her phone buzzed, breaking her trance.

Ethan Numan.

She swiped to answer, raising her voice slightly over the hum of the engines. "Ethan. What's up?"

"Hey, Molly," Ethan said, his tone carefully neutral but carrying an undercurrent of unease. "Figured I'd catch you mid-air—less chance for distractions."

She smirked faintly. "Or escape?"

"You said it, not me." His chuckle was short, but Molly could sense something heavier beneath it. "Look, I wanted to run something by you. It's about your dad."

Molly sat up straighter. "Okay… what about him?"

Ethan hesitated, and she could almost hear him debating whether to continue. Finally, he said, "A couple of days ago, your dad came to me with a hypothetical. No restrictions. No regulations. Unlimited resources. He wanted to know how quickly I could deliver the next phase of Project Milo under those conditions."

Molly frowned, the words sinking in slowly. "And what did you say?"

"Well, first, I told him it's a completely absurd scenario. No restrictions? That's not even in the realm of possibility. But he kept pushing, so I gave him an answer just to end the conversation. A year, maybe less. Honestly, I thought it was a rhetorical exercise."

Her father's relentless determination was nothing new, but something in Ethan's voice made her stomach tighten. "But now you're not so sure."

"That's putting it lightly." Ethan exhaled sharply. "Your dad can be… persuasive. And by persuasive, I mean borderline terrifying when he wants something. I just wanted to ask if he's said anything to you about it—any hint that he's planning something bigger?"

Molly rubbed her temple. "No, nothing like that. I mean, he's always thinking ten steps ahead, but if he was planning something that extreme, I think I'd know."

"I hope so," Ethan said, though his voice didn't sound entirely convinced. "He's just… got me spooked. This kind of conversation isn't exactly casual dinner talk, you know?"

"I'll talk to him," Molly promised. "Get a sense of where his head's at."

"Thanks." There was a pause, the hum of the engines filling the space between them. "There's something else… but this stays between us."

Molly arched an eyebrow. "Alright, now you're making me nervous. What is it?"

"It's something Dr. Park flagged about Project Heal," Ethan began, his voice lowering as if someone might overhear. "We've been seeing some… anomalies in the data. Weird stuff."

"What kind of weird?"

Ethan hesitated. "I shouldn't say more until I know for sure. Just—when I figure it out, I'll let you know. For now, just keep an eye out, okay?"

Molly's mind raced, but she bit back the flood of questions forming on her tongue. "Fine. But when you have answers, I want them."

"You'll be the first to know," Ethan assured her.

Molly moved to hang up. But as she pulled the phone away, she realized the line was still active.

"Ethan?" she called out.

No response.

She frowned, about to end the call, when she heard a muffled voice. It was Ethan—talking to someone else.

"…Milo, I can't just ask her!" Ethan's voice was low but distinctly flustered. "She's not just anyone—she's Molly Scent."

A muffled response followed, but Molly couldn't make out the words.

"I know I said she's amazing. That doesn't mean I'm… Milo, stop. This isn't happening."

Molly raised an eyebrow, a grin already forming. "Ethan?"

A pause. Then the sound of rustling. Ethan's voice came through, stiff and formal. "Uh, Molly. Yes, I'm still here. Sorry about that."

Molly leaned back in her seat, letting the silence draw out.

"Everything okay?" she asked innocently.

"Yes. Yes, fine," Ethan replied, far too quickly. Then, after an awkward pause, he blurted, "Would you like to have dinner sometime?"

Molly blinked, biting her lip to stifle a laugh. "Dinner?"

"Yes. I mean, if you're interested. If you're not, that's fine. Actually, you probably shouldn't. Milo said I should ask, but he's—not great at these things. And you're… well, you. I mean, you're Mr. Scent's daughter, and this is—oh, never mind."

"Ethan—"

"It was a bad idea. Forget I asked. Goodbye, Molly." And just like that, the line went dead.

For a moment, Molly stared at her phone, torn between amusement and disbelief. Finally, shaking her head, she typed out a message:

8:00 PM tomorrow. The Bistro on Main.

She hit send, a small, satisfied smile spreading across her face. You were right, Milo. He just needed a push.

As the call ended, Molly stared at the phone in her hand, the unease in Ethan's voice still lingering. She glanced out the window again, but the familiar scenery did little to quiet her thoughts.

Her father's relentless ambition. Ethan's cryptic warning. The strange sense that something bigger was brewing beneath the surface.

#

Another helicopter took Molly the short hop from the private airport to the Scent estate. The rotors slowed as they began their descent, the sprawling mansion stretched out like a shadow, its manicured lawns and modern architecture bathed in the amber glow of dusk.

The helipad came into view, and Molly's pulse quickened.

The moment the skids touched the ground, she was out, her heels clicking against the concrete as she made her way toward the house. The staff knew better than to appear on this day, and the mansion felt eerily still as she entered, the air heavy with an unspoken tension.

Molly paused at the bottom of the sweeping staircase, her gaze drifting toward the west wing—the part of the house her father always retreated to on this day.

Her breath caught in her throat, and for a moment, she hesitated.

"Dad," she whispered to herself, then began climbing the stairs, each step echoing softly in the empty house.

The room was dim, the only light spilling in from the setting sun through the half-drawn blinds. Nolan sat on the edge of the king-sized bed in his private sanctuary, a place no one entered but him. He leaned forward, elbows on his knees, his hands cradling a small, worn velvet box.

Inside, the necklace gleamed faintly in the fading light. Two delicate pendants hung from the chain, the letters F and G—simple, unassuming, and loaded with a weight that pressed against his chest every time he looked at them.

A quiet laugh, more bitter than amused, escaped his lips. Absurd nickname. But it was her way. Rebecca had always known how to take his too-serious mind and remind him of the beauty in nonsense, the kind that made life worth living.

They'd been sitting on the couch in their tiny apartment, a pair of mismatched mugs on the coffee table and an open laptop between them. He was deep into a coding problem, muttering about variables, when Rebecca wandered in wearing one of his oversized T-shirts, her hair a messy halo.

"Stop," she'd said, plopping down beside him.

"Stop what?" he replied without looking up.

"Being so… you." She leaned her head against his shoulder. "I've been thinking."

"Dangerous," he teased, finally glancing at her.

She smacked his arm lightly. "You should feed all the children in Africa."

Nolan blinked at her, baffled. "What?"

"Jesus fed 5,000 people with some fish and bread, right? You've got this brain of yours, all these fancy algorithms. You should figure out how to feed all the children in Africa."

For a moment, the absurdity of her suggestion rendered him speechless. Then he saw the earnestness in her big, brown eyes, and he laughed—a deep, genuine laugh that shook loose the tension in his shoulders.

"It's a parable," he said, wiping a tear of laughter from the corner of his eye. "Not a business plan. You don't even go to church, any church, ever."

Rebecca just smiled, wrapping her arms around his neck. "Doesn't mean the children aren't hungry. You've got time. Start now."

A few days later, she gave him the necklace. "So, you never forget," she'd said, her grin mischievous. "You'll always be my Fish Guy."

The memory shifted—turning darker, colder. The sterile scent of the hospital filled his nostrils, and the beeping of machines rang in his ears. Rebecca had been laughing that morning, full of excitement as they packed for the hospital. By evening, the laughter had stopped, replaced by the panicked voices of doctors and nurses.

"Mr. Scent," one of them said, their face a blur in his mind. "We're so sorry."

They handed him Molly—tiny, red-faced, wailing. A miracle and a curse all at once. He'd stared at her, unable to feel anything but numbness.

For years, Rebecca's smile haunted him, growing sharper every time he tried to push it away. The necklace stayed in its box, untouched, until one particularly bad night. Molly was still young, asleep in her room, oblivious to the storm raging in her father's mind.

He'd opened the box, pulling out the chain and holding it up to the light. The letters glinted like an accusation, dragging him back to the kitchen where she'd first called him Fish Guy, her laughter

echoing in his ears.
Then his gaze fell on the gun.
He didn't remember picking it up, didn't remember sitting at the edge of the bed, spinning the chamber. All he remembered was the click of the hammer falling on an empty round. Again. And again.

The next morning, Molly found him slumped over, the gun still in his hand, the necklace tangled in his fingers. She didn't say a word, just took the gun and left the room.

Nolan's hand trembled as he closed the box and set it on the bedside table.
His phone buzzed, breaking the heavy silence, a text message from Molly: On my way.
He stared at the screen for a long moment before setting the phone aside. Standing, he walked to the window and looked out over the manicured grounds of his estate. The sun was low, its last rays painting the horizon in gold and crimson.
Somewhere in the distance, he thought he heard birds chirping. Rebecca loved feeding the birds.
He closed his eyes and let the sound take him back, just for a moment.
When he opened them again, the light was fading, and the room was darker than before. He turned back toward the bed, his gaze falling once more on the velvet box.
"Fish Guy," he whispered, his voice barely audible.

#

The door creaked softly as Molly pushed it open, stepping inside with a caution that felt almost ritualistic. The room was bathed in the soft amber glow of a single lamp, its light spilling over the neatly arranged artefacts of a life lost too soon—Rebecca's favorite books, a scarf draped over the back of a chair, framed photos capturing fleeting moments of joy.

Nolan sat in the corner, his back to the door, more relaxed than Molly expected. He wasn't clutching a glass of whiskey or staring blankly into space like he had on this day in previous years. Instead, he seemed thoughtful, almost calm, his gaze fixed on an old necklace dangling from his fingers—the letters F and G catching the light.

"You look so much like her," Nolan said without turning, his voice quiet but steady.

Molly froze for a moment, then stepped further into the room. "You've said that before."

He finally turned, scanning her face as though seeing it anew. "But you're not her. You've got her eyes, her grace… but everything else, that's me. The drive, the stubbornness, the way you bite your lip when you're calculating your next move." He paused, his expression softening. "Maybe if your mother had survived, she would have brought more of herself out in you."

Molly felt a pang in her chest, the weight of what could have been. "Do you ever wish…?" she started, but he cut her off gently.

"Every day," Nolan said, his voice dropping to a whisper.

They stood in silence, the unspoken words between them heavy in the air. Then Molly's gaze dropped to the necklace in his hand.

"Is today the day you finally tell me what F G stands for?"

Nolan's lips curved into a faint smile. He looked at the necklace as though it held the answer to a question he'd been avoiding for years. "Fish Guy," he said after a long beat.

Molly blinked. "Fish Guy?"

He nodded, chuckling softly. "Your mother's name for me. She gave me this after she decided I was going to feed all the starving children in Africa."

Molly frowned. "What?"

"She had this wild, beautiful heart," Nolan said, his voice growing wistful. "One day, she was reading an article about famine. It broke her. She couldn't stop crying. The next day, she told me I was going to feed all those children. She was so certain, so… determined. Said I could figure it out, like Jesus with the loaves and fishes."

Molly's eyes widened. "And you didn't say no?"

"How could I?" Nolan's smile was tinged with melancholy. "She was sitting there, in her underwear, her hair a mess, looking more beautiful than I'd ever seen her. For a moment, I almost believed it too. That I could change the world."

Molly studied him. "Why don't you?" she asked, her voice soft but insistent. "Why don't we?"

For a fleeting second, Nolan saw Rebecca in her. The same fiery conviction, the same unshakable belief in doing good. His breath caught, and for a moment, he wanted to say yes.

But the moment passed.

He shook his head, his gaze hardening. "It's not that simple, Molly. Life's not about parables or miracles. It's about chance. I had a school friend whose father was killed in a car accident when we were kids. The man was just walking across the street, and out of nowhere—gone. Some people are born into wealth, some into poverty, and most fall somewhere in between. There's no justice in it. It's just the way things are."

Molly wasn't ready to give up. "But doesn't that mean we should try to even things out? To do something good?"

Nolan sighed, his expression turning pensive. "Those are man-made concepts. Justice. Fairness. Doing good. They don't exist in nature. After your mother died… if they ever mattered to me, they stopped being a priority."

Molly stepped closer, her voice quieter now. "Then why Project Heal? Why Project Milo? What's the real goal, Dad?"

For the first time that night, Nolan's composure cracked. His eyes glistened with an emotion she couldn't name—grief, hope, or something more profound. When he spoke, his voice was raw.

"Immortality," he said simply. "Overcoming death."

Molly's breath hitched. The weight of the word hung in the air between them, vast and incomprehensible. For a second, she couldn't find the words, couldn't even process what he had just said.

Nolan looked back at the necklace in his hand, his grip tightening around it. "That's what it's always been about, Molly. Not saving the world. Just… not losing everything again."

Molly stared at her father, her heart heavy with the realization of how deeply her mother's loss had shaped him. For all his ambition, for all his ruthlessness, this—this was the man at his core.

But before she could say anything, Nolan stood abruptly, slipping the necklace into his pocket.

"You should rest," he said, his tone brisk again. "It's been a long day."

Molly nodded mutely, her thoughts a storm as she watched him leave the room.

#

Molly sat across from her father at the long, polished breakfast table. The light streaming through the mansion's tall windows cast a soft glow over the array of untouched dishes between them. Nolan, dressed impeccably as always, sipped his black coffee with an air of detachment. Despite the casual setting, his presence filled the room.

She stirred her tea absently, gathering her thoughts. The necklace revelation had lingered in her mind, a rare glimpse into a side of her father she barely knew. But that glimmer of humanity had quickly retreated, replaced by the calculating figure now sitting before her.

"You said it's about not losing everything again," she said finally. "But what does that actually mean? What are you really trying to achieve?"

Nolan turned slowly, the contemplative air from earlier hardening into his usual composed, almost impenetrable demeanor. His voice was cool, detached.

"I've seen the world for what it is, Molly. A place of chaos, chance, and raw power. The strong survive, the weak get crushed, and fairness is nothing more than a story we tell ourselves to sleep better at night." He met her gaze. "Your mother believed in fairness. She believed in miracles. And look where that got her."

Molly flinched at the edge in his tone but held her ground. "So, what then? You're trying to create some perfect world where you never lose anything again?"

He chuckled, low and bitter. "Perfect? No, Molly. There's no such thing. What I'm creating is order. Stability. A world where those who matter, those who can do something with the time they have, aren't held back by the chaos of the masses."

Molly's stomach twisted at his words, but she pressed on. "And Project Milo? That's not about order. That's something else."

His gaze sharpened, and for a moment, she thought he might dodge the question. But then his lips curved into a faint, almost imperceptible smile.

"Immortality," he said simply. "Not just for me, but for the best of us. For the ones who should endure."

Molly's breath caught. The starkness of his ambition hit her like a physical blow. "You really think that's possible?"

Nolan's expression remained calm, almost serene. "If it's not, then why are we here? Why build, innovate, conquer? Why have civilization at all if not to push the boundaries of what's possible? Your mother… she believed in miracles. I don't. I believe in results."

Molly wanted to argue, to push back, but something in his tone—the absolute certainty—stopped her. Instead, she shifted the topic, though her voice had lost its earlier conviction. "So, the conversation with Ethan about no restrictions… what was that about?"

Nolan's lips tightened, and for a brief moment, his mask slipped, revealing a flicker of annoyance. "Ethan's brilliant, but he gets too caught up in rules and processes. I asked him to consider possibilities, not limitations. That's all. I have a plan, Molly, and I'm not asking him to do anything illegal."

It was a vague reassurance, but Molly knew better than to press further. She shifted gears again. "Ethan mentioned some strange data from Project Heal. Something about the subjects registering as brain dead? Do you know anything about that?"

Nolan feigned mild interest, though his tone remained indifferent. "I don't, but I'm sure the scientists will figure it out. That's their job."

Molly frowned, her frustration simmering just beneath the surface. "You're not even curious?"

He shrugged. "Curiosity is a distraction. I pay people to solve problems. I expect them to deliver."

Realizing she'd hit another wall, Molly sighed. "I need to get back to Harmony Falls."

Nolan nodded, walking her to the door with the air of a man who had already moved on to his next thought. "Keep an eye on Jansen," he said as she stepped out. "He's trouble, even if he doesn't realize it yet."

Molly gave a faint nod and left, her mind spinning with the conversation they'd just had.

As the door clicked shut, Nolan's calm facade dropped. He crossed briskly to his desk, opened a hidden drawer, and retrieved an encrypted phone. Dialing swiftly, he waited for the line to connect.

"Lucas," he said, his voice sharp and commanding. "I need the full details of a recent conversation between Park and Ethan. Pull everything from the lab's audio logs."

"Yes, sir," Lucas replied without hesitation. "Anything specific I should look for?"

"Anything related to strange data readings," Nolan said. "And start exploring replacements for Ethan Numan."

A pause. "Replacements? Sir, Ethan's work with Milo is deeply personal. No one else has his connection to the project—or his brother."

Nolan's jaw tightened. "Leave that to me. Just find me options."

"Yes, Mr. Scent."

Nolan hung up and leaned back in his chair, his fingers steepled beneath his chin. His mind raced, calculating his next steps. The world didn't run on miracles, he thought. It ran on power—and he intended to wield it like no one ever had.

Molly leaned back in the plush leather seat of the Scent Technologies car, her gaze fixed on the streets passing in a blur. Her father's words from breakfast lingered in her mind, heavy yet familiar, like a recurring dream she couldn't shake. The Fish Guy story had stayed with her longer than she cared to admit, gnawing at the edges of her thoughts.

But as the car approached the airfield, another thought interrupted her reverie—her dinner plans with Ethan.

She grabbed her phone, quickly scrolling to his number. Before she could overthink it, she pressed call.

"Ethan Numan," came his slightly breathless greeting.

"Hi, Ethan. It's Molly," she said, smiling at how formal he sounded, as though she might be calling to deliver a verdict on his career.

There was a brief pause, followed by the sound of papers rustling. "Oh, Molly! Hi! Everything okay?"

"Everything's fine," she assured him, stifling a laugh at his nervous tone. "I just realized I might have to reschedule our dinner tonight. My flight to Harmony Falls is cutting it a bit close."

"Oh… right. No problem at all," Ethan replied, a little too quickly. "I mean, I understand. You're busy, and—"

"But," she interrupted, her tone teasing, "how about brunch instead? I can make some time before I fly."

"Brunch?" he repeated, the word landing awkwardly in the silence. "Uh… I'd like to, but I can't really leave Milo alone on such short notice. He's been… unpredictable lately."

Molly smirked. "Then I'll come to you. Coffee and donuts on the rooftop garden."

There was another pause, long enough for her to picture him fumbling for an excuse.

"You really don't have to—"

"Ethan," she said firmly, cutting him off, "do you like maple-glazed donuts or not?"

A soft laugh escaped him, more genuine this time. "I do."

"Good. I'll be there in thirty minutes," Molly declared, her grin widening.

"Wait—Molly—"

"See you soon," she said, hanging up before he could protest further.

She leaned toward the driver. "Take a quick detour. I need to pick up some donuts."

Settling back into her seat, Molly let out a small, private laugh. It had been a long time since anyone treated her as more than Nolan Scent's daughter. With Ethan, there was no agenda, no calculated manoeuvring—just unvarnished awkwardness that felt… real.

She liked that.

She liked him.

#

The rooftop garden of Ethan and Milo's apartment was as serene as she remembered, a lush oasis high above the city. The late morning sun cast a golden glow over the plants, the faint scent of lavender and rosemary mingling with the breeze.

Ethan was already there, fidgeting with a small coffee setup at the table, looking more nervous than she'd expected.

"You weren't kidding about being quick," he said as she approached, holding up the box of donuts like a prize.

"I never joke about donuts," Molly replied, setting the box on the table. "Maple-glazed, just as requested."

Ethan smiled, slightly sheepish, as he poured her a cup of coffee. "So… welcome back to the garden."

Molly took a seat, savoring the rich aroma as she sipped. They sat in comfortable silence for a moment, the sound of the city below a faint hum. Ethan fidgeted with his coffee cup, his gaze flickering toward her before quickly darting away.

"You're quiet," Molly said, tilting her head. "Second thoughts about brunch?"

"No, not at all," Ethan said quickly. "It's just… I've been thinking about Harmony Falls. You've got your dad's big plans for the future on one side, and then Jansen talking about dinosaurs and extinction on the other. That's… a lot to navigate."

Molly chuckled, leaning back. "It is ironic, isn't it? One man building a future for humanity, the other trying to remind us not to repeat the past. People are drawn to Jansen. He makes you feel like being human means something."

Ethan nodded, his brow furrowed. "And what about you? Where do you land between those two?"

Molly hesitated, caught off guard by the question. Most people assumed they knew where she stood—firmly in her father's corner. But Ethan wasn't most people. He wasn't asking as Nolan Scent's employee or as someone looking for leverage.

He was asking her.

"A lot of people agree with Jansen," she said finally. "He talks about humanity like it's worth saving, not just upgrading. It's hard not to respect that."

Ethan studied her, his expression thoughtful. "And you? What do you think?"

She met his gaze, appreciating the sincerity in his question. "How about I share my views over dinner sometime?" she offered, her tone light but her smile genuine.

Ethan blinked, clearly caught off guard. "I'd… like that."

"Good," Molly said, taking a bite of her donut. "I'll let you know when I'm back from Harmony Falls."

The tension that had hung between them earlier seemed to dissolve, replaced by something warmer, easier. They continued talking, the conversation flowing naturally. Ethan opened up about his work with Milo, sharing stories that revealed his passion and his humanity.

Molly found herself laughing more than she had in weeks, the weight of her usual responsibilities momentarily lifting.

As the sun climbed higher, casting dappled light across the garden, Molly felt a sense of calm she hadn't experienced in a long time.

She wasn't sure what this was between her and Ethan, but she wanted to find out.

"Thanks for the coffee," she said as she stood, brushing crumbs from her lap.

"Thanks for the donuts," Ethan replied, his smile shy but warm.

Molly lingered for a moment, her hand resting on the back of her chair. "See you soon, Ethan."

"Yeah," he said softly. "See you soon."

As she descended the stairs, Molly couldn't help but smile. The rooftop garden, the coffee, the conversation—it all felt like a small slice of normalcy in a life that was anything but.

And for the first time in a while, she allowed herself to enjoy it.

# STAGE 4: MASS EXTINCTION – SOCIETAL COLLAPSE

## Stage 4: Mass Extinction – Societal Collapse (macro view)

The asteroid's impact had already altered the landscape.
Now came the aftershocks—the tremors that shattered the structures of society, leaving individuals scrambling to find meaning in the rubble.

It wasn't just about jobs anymore. AI wasn't merely a technological shift; it was a reordering of human purpose. Those who once formed the backbone of industry, commerce, and services found themselves obsolete. Their roles as workers, providers, and contributors to the economy had collapsed.

But survival required more than income.
It required identity.
And identity was eroding.

**Mass Job Displacement & Class Collapse**
AI is projected to displace millions of workers annually—erasing entire professions:

- Truck drivers
- Legal assistants
- Mid-tier accountants

"AI is no longer replacing jobs—it's erasing entire career paths," Brookings analysts have warned. (Brookings)

The economic gap between the AI-augmented workforce and the un-augmented is expected to grow wider than at any period in modern history. Augmented workers—those with neural implants, bio-optimizations, and algorithmic enhancements—are projected to out-earn their non-augmented counterparts by a significant margin. (McKinsey)

For the rest, the economy will have simply passed them by.

**Crime & Social Unrest**

The human cost is already reflected in the streets.

Regions with high displacement are experiencing increased theft and vandalism. Political instability is spreading as AI-driven inequality fuels unrest in multiple countries—the largest wave of political instability in over a century.

"AI-driven economic inequality has become a leading cause of civil unrest worldwide," Brookings analysts have warned. (Brookings)

**Erosion of Democracy**

Governments are increasingly deferring key policy decisions to AI systems. Political campaigns are now modeled on algorithmic voter sentiment analysis. Economic policy is being drafted based on predictive AI market simulations. Even foreign policy is being shaped by AI-generated conflict models.

"AI now dictates economic and political outcomes," The Atlantic reported. "The era of human-led governance is closing." (The Atlantic)

Governments no longer govern. They manage.

**Rise of AI Dependency**

For most, survival now depends on compliance with the system.

A growing share of the population in developed nations relies on AI-driven welfare systems for job placement, financial planning, and even emotional support. AI-generated therapy programs have replaced human counselors. Automated investment platforms control personal wealth. Algorithm-driven social networks dictate emotional well-being.

"AI dependency is not just financial—it's emotional and existential," the Global AI Society Index noted. (Global AI Society Index)

The world is no longer built for humans—it is built for those who can sync with the machine.

**Ghosts in Their Own World**

For the un-augmented—for those who resist the chips, the implants, the integrations—society has no place left for them.

They are ghosts in their own world, wandering through a system that has moved beyond them.

### ***Stage 4: Mass Extinction - Societal Collapse (micro view)***

*The Harmony Falls train station used to be bustling. Morning commuters packed shoulder to shoulder, waving to neighbors, grabbing quick coffees from the small kiosk run by Aiden Chen's family for nearly three decades. Now, the platform was empty, the only sound the occasional creak of the wind brushing through the neglected beams of the overhang.*

*Greg Taylor sat on one of the benches, his broad shoulders hunched against the chill of the evening. His work boots, scuffed and worn, rested flat on the concrete, the steel toe catching the dim light of the flickering overhead bulb. He held a manila envelope in his hands, crumpled and dog-eared from hours of nervous gripping.*

*Greg had worked in construction since he was eighteen. He wasn't just a worker--he was a foreman, the guy who knew how to read the plans, lead the crew, handle the unexpected. For years, he had taken pride in building homes, schools, offices--watching something rise from nothing.*

*But the AI-driven machines changed all that. They didn't miss measurements, didn't call in sick, didn't argue about overtime. Automated construction crews could lay foundations and erect entire buildings in a fraction of the time, with none of the cost or hassle of human labor.*

*Greg's company had held on longer than most, but the contracts dried up as competitors adopted AI. Three months ago, Greg had been laid off with the rest of his crew. He had tried to find work--anything to keep the bills paid--but even the roofing jobs and handyman gigs were disappearing, overtaken by robots and automated systems.*

*Now the manila envelope in his pocket contained his final eviction notice. The house he had built with his own hands was no longer his.*

*Inside the kiosk, Aiden Chen shuffled papers, his back stiff from sitting on a wobbly stool for hours. The family business had been his pride, but even pride couldn't fight the algorithms. When construction jobs like Greg's dried up, so did the workers who stopped in for coffee and bagels before heading to the job sites.*

*Aiden had tried adapting. He added vending machines with pre-programmed AI assistants for "efficiency," but even those were now gathering dust. The only customers he saw were Greg and a few other displaced workers, nursing watery cups of coffee as they stared blankly at the tracks.*

*"Greg," Aiden called as the man approached the kiosk. "The usual?"*

*Greg nodded silently. Aiden poured the coffee.*

*"You know, I don't think I'll be back tomorrow."*

*Aiden frowned, setting the pot down. "What do you mean?"*

*Greg hesitated, his gaze fixed on the floor. "They're taking the house, Aiden. No point in sticking around."*

*The two men fell into a heavy silence, the kind that came when there was nothing left to say. Aiden understood more than he let on. He and his wife had burned through their savings trying to keep the kiosk alive. The landlord had been patient, but patience was running thin.*

*"You ever think it wasn't supposed to be like this?" Aiden asked finally, his voice barely above a whisper.*

*Greg snorted. "Supposed to be? Nah. No one cared about what was 'supposed to be' when they brought in the machines. They care about speed, cost, and nothing else."*

*Aiden nodded, his hand gripping the edge of the counter as if steadying himself. "You think there's a way out of this?"*

*Greg laughed bitterly. "Not for us. Maybe for the ones in the suits, running the whole show."*

*The train arrived, its automated systems perfectly aligned with the empty station. Greg boarded without looking back, carrying nothing but the envelope in his pocket.*

*Aiden watched the train glide away, its mechanical precision a painful contrast to the human chaos it left behind. He stayed behind the counter for a long time after Greg left, his hands trembling slightly as he stared at the empty tracks. The kiosk felt smaller than ever, and the future felt impossibly far away.*

*The extinction wasn't immediate. It wasn't a meteor smashing into the earth with fiery finality. It was the train station growing quieter. The coffee growing colder. The laughter of friends fading into silence.*

*For Greg Taylor and Aiden Chen, the world had already ended--quietly, efficiently, and without a single human hand.*

# CHAPTER 13

The early sunlight cast sharp angles across Lucas Bennett's office as he reviewed the day's agenda. The Harmony Falls PR event was poised to showcase Scent Technologies' successes, a perfect counter-narrative to the growing unrest in the country. Yet the uneasy hum in his chest told him the morning wouldn't go as smoothly as he'd planned.

A sharp knock interrupted his thoughts. Eric Summers strode in without waiting, his expression tight. His usual smugness was replaced by something closer to worry, and Lucas sat up straighter.
"What now, Eric?" Lucas asked, irritation creeping into his tone.
Eric closed the door firmly before speaking. "It's Jansen. He visited one of the families yesterday. Spent hours talking to them, and from what I hear, he got pretty deep. The Hawkins, I think."
Lucas's eyes narrowed. "The Hawkins. That's the young couple with the sick infant?"
"Exactly," Eric said, crossing his arms. "And the timing's bad. Jansen's been gathering ammo, and if he brings them into the spotlight at the event today, it could blow up in our faces."
Lucas tapped his pen on the desk, considering. "What kind of ammo?"
Eric shrugged. "Probably the usual: exploitation, control, your chips are the devil kind of thing. The problem is, this family's sympathetic as hell. If they stand up and side with Jansen, it could go viral in minutes."
Lucas leaned back, his mind racing. "Do we know what they said to him?"
"No," Eric admitted. "But the way he's been moving, he's going to try something big."
Lucas exhaled sharply, processing. Jansen was unpredictable, but

this wasn't just an academic stunt—it was targeted. If he was setting them up for a blow in public, they needed to preempt it before the first camera went live. He set his pen down and pushed back from the desk.

"Then we need to make our move first," he said. "Get Dr. Marks in here. Now."

Dr. Angela Marks entered Lucas's office, her crisp lab coat as meticulously pressed as her speech. Unlike Eric, she exuded no warmth, no camaraderie—just the cool efficiency of a professional doing her job.

She placed a file on his desk. "Lucas. You wanted to see me?"

Lucas flipped it open, scanning the contents. "The Hawkins family. Tell me what we're dealing with."

Dr. Marks adjusted her glasses. "Joshua and Julie Hawkins. Both employed at Delta Precision Manufacturing. They're on the replacement list due to low productivity scores and skill redundancy."

Lucas barely glanced up. "And the baby?"

Dr. Marks's tone remained clinical. "Severe brain malformation. Without intervention, the child will never develop motor skills or independent function. Life expectancy is limited."

Lucas's expression darkened. "But the neural chip could change that."

"Correct." She folded her hands neatly. "An intracranial chip would bypass the damaged areas, allowing for near-normal development. It's a textbook case for demonstrating the chip's potential. However, the parents have been resistant. They've voiced strong anti-Scent sentiments."

Lucas leaned back, the beginnings of a plan forming. "And Jansen spent time with them yesterday?"

Dr. Marks gave a small nod. "According to the data, yes. He's likely reinforcing their resistance."

Lucas exhaled slowly, his mind already turning. "Then we need to change the narrative." He shut the file and looked up. "Schedule a meeting with the Hawkins. I'll handle it personally."

The morning sunlight struggled to filter through the thin curtains of the Hawkins' modest living room. Josh sat at the small kitchen table, nursing a lukewarm cup of coffee that he'd reheated twice. His hands were clasped tightly around the mug, his knuckles white. Across from him, Julie cradled their infant son, rocking gently as the baby let out soft, intermittent cries. Her eyes were bloodshot, and she wore the exhaustion of too many sleepless nights.

"It feels like we're just… waiting," Josh muttered, breaking the heavy silence. "Waiting for them to tell us we're done. That we're next."

Julie glanced at him, her own despair mirrored in his face. "You mean fired?"

Josh nodded, staring into the dark liquid in his mug. "Laid off, replaced, whatever they call it now. Doesn't make a difference."

Julie adjusted the baby in her arms, her voice trembling. "Jansen said there might be a way to fight back, but what does that even mean? A protest? A petition? Like any of that's going to stop them."

Josh leaned back in his chair, running a hand through his unkempt hair. "It's not about fighting back, Julie. It's about surviving. We've got to figure out what we're going to do if—when—it happens."

Julie's grip on the baby tightened. "What about him, Josh? He's not going to get better on his own. And we can't afford the treatments. We can't even afford another specialist appointment."

Josh's jaw clenched. "You think I don't know that?" His voice came out rough with frustration. "I look at him and I feel… useless. Like I'm already failing him."

Julie's expression softened. She reached across the table, placing her hand on his. "You're not failing him. You're not failing us."

Josh shook his head, his eyes glassy. "I'm supposed to protect you, take care of my family. But how am I supposed to do that when the rug's being pulled out from under us? When every job out there is being replaced by some damn machine?"

Julie rocked their baby a little more firmly, trying to soothe him. "I don't know, Josh," she whispered. "I just want us to have a chance. A real chance. Is that too much to ask?"

The baby let out a small wail, and Julie sighed, pressing her cheek to his head. "And he didn't sleep again last night," she added softly. "I'm scared, Josh. For all of us."

Josh exhaled heavily and stood, pacing the small space. "We'll figure it out. Somehow."

Julie watched him, tears welling in her eyes. "We've been saying that for weeks. What if there's no figuring it out this time?"

Before Josh could answer, the landline phone rang. The sharp sound broke through the thick tension in the room. Julie's brow furrowed as she stood, still holding the baby, and walked over to answer.

"Hello?" she said cautiously.

"Mrs. Hawkins? This is Dr. Marks, from Scent Technologies," came a smooth, professional voice on the other end.

Julie stiffened, glancing at Josh, who immediately froze mid-pace. "Yes… what is this about?"

Dr. Marks continued, her tone even and businesslike. "We've reviewed your family's case, and we'd like to extend an invitation to meet with Lucas Bennett this morning. He'd like to discuss some potential solutions for your current situation."

Julie's heart thudded in her chest. "Solutions? What kind of solutions?"

"All of that will be covered in the meeting," Dr. Marks said with practiced neutrality. "We believe this could be a significant opportunity for your family. Would you be able to come to the Harmony Falls Community Center at ten o'clock?"

Julie hesitated, her gaze darting to Josh. His jaw was tight, his face unreadable, but he gave her a small, reluctant nod.

"We'll be there," she said finally.

"Wonderful," Dr. Marks replied. "We'll see you soon."

Julie hung up the phone and turned to Josh, her expression a mix of apprehension and fragile hope. "They want to meet with us."

Josh crossed his arms, his skepticism clear. "And what exactly do they want to offer us?"

"I don't know," Julie admitted. "But what choice do we have? We've got to at least hear them out."

Josh sighed deeply and sat back down at the table. "Yeah," he said quietly. "I guess we do."

The tension in the air was thick as Joshua and Julie Hawkins sat stiffly across from Lucas Bennett. Julie cradled their baby, her protective hold signaling her distrust of the man in front of her. Josh's jaw was set, his hands gripping his knees as though holding himself back from lunging across the desk.

"We're not here to listen to some sales pitch," Josh said bluntly. "We know what you're about."

Lucas offered a conciliatory smile. "Josh, Julie, I understand your skepticism. And I understand you've been speaking with Professor Jansen. He's a thoughtful man, but he doesn't have all the facts."

Julie's eyes narrowed. "He has enough to know what you're doing here."

Lucas leaned forward, his tone softening. "What I'm doing here is offering you a chance to save your child."

The room fell silent. Julie's grip on the baby tightened, and Josh's expression wavered for a split second before hardening again.

"I've reviewed your situation," Lucas continued. "You're about to lose your jobs. Without income, you can't afford the medical care your child needs. And even if you could, conventional treatments won't give your baby the life he deserves. But the neural chip can."

Julie's voice cracked as she spoke. "We don't want some… experiment done on our baby."

"This isn't an experiment," Lucas said smoothly. "It's a proven technology. And it's not just for your child. The chip would secure your positions at Delta Precision, guaranteeing your family's stability. No layoffs. No uncertainty. A future."

Josh shook his head, but his resolve was faltering. "You make it sound so simple."

"It is simple," Lucas said, his voice soft but firm. "Your child's life depends on this. What parent wouldn't do everything they could?"

Julie looked down at the baby, her tears falling silently. Josh rubbed his face, torn between his principles and his desperation.

"What's the catch?" Josh finally asked, his voice hoarse.

Lucas leaned back, his smile returning. "No catch. Just a request. At the PR event today, Professor Jansen is likely to make some accusations about Scent Technologies. All I need you to do is tell the truth—how we've helped your family."

Julie looked up, her expression conflicted. "And if we don't?"

For a fleeting moment, Lucas's gaze hardened before he said, "If you don't feel you can say Scent Technologies is helping you, I fail to see how we can provide the medical treatments for Joey and the job opportunities for both of you."

Julie hesitated. "There was other stuff about our friends. Professor Jansen spoke to us about how they have changed after having the chips implanted."

"Maybe there is some truth in that. I'm not the scientist here, neither are you. Let them speak for themselves. If they are unhappy or have concerns, they can stand up and speak. You have to do what's best for your family."

Josh and Julie exchanged a long, silent look. Finally, Josh exhaled and nodded. "We'll do it."

Lucas smiled. "You're making the right choice." As they left, a flicker of satisfaction passed through him. Jansen believed he was going to expose Scent Technologies. If he could have been in the room just now, he might understand there was nothing to expose. People always act in their own self-interest. It's the most fundamental law of survival.

The Hawkins were doing it, and so was Nolan—but on a grander scale, not for one child and two jobs, but for all the children whose parents needed jobs. What Scent Technologies was doing with its

AI technology was akin to the invention of electricity, but with exponentially faster impact and benefit to corporate America. Nolan's neural chip program was ensuring it would work for everyone. The natural order of the best—by implication, the wealthiest—having the most would be preserved.

Harmony Falls would be the catalyst for cementing America's AI-driven future. Lucas wasn't going to leave anything to chance. He made a call.

"Molly, thanks for picking up. I know you're with Jansen, but I need a quick favor."

"Not with him yet, on my way to meet him now. What kind of favor?"

"There's a young family, the Hawkins, they're… in a tough spot," Lucas said, carefully choosing his words. "You know how it is in Harmony Falls. Layoffs, job insecurity. They're just trying to figure things out, and I'm working on helping them. But if Jansen brings them up at the event later, it's only going to make things harder for them."

Molly frowned, her brow furrowing. "Harder how? Are they in trouble?"

Lucas hesitated, then sighed, pitching his voice to sound almost weary. "Not trouble exactly. Let's just say they're caught between a rock and a hard place. And Jansen—well, he doesn't always consider the collateral damage of his grandstanding. If he makes the Hawkins family a centerpiece of his speech, it's not going to help anyone. Least of all them."

"I don't know, Lucas. You know how Jansen is. He's not exactly the type to hold back."

"Which is why I'm asking you," Lucas pressed, his tone softening. "You have his ear, Molly. Just… talk to him. Ask him to steer clear of the Hawkins. Tell him I'm trying to figure out a way to help them, but it's delicate. It's not going to do any good if they get dragged into the spotlight."

Molly sighed, leaning back against her seat. "Lucas, this doesn't sound like you. Since when are you delicate?"

Lucas's smile was audible through the phone. "I have my moments. Look, Molly, you care about people, right? About making a difference? This is a chance to do that. Keep Jansen focused on the big picture. The Hawkins family isn't it."

Molly's grip on the phone tightened. "I'll talk to him. But I'm not making any promises."

"That's all I'm asking," Lucas said smoothly. "Thanks, Molly. I owe you one."

She ended the call, her mind spinning. Lucas Bennett wasn't the type to owe favors, and his sudden appeal to her sense of compassion left her unsettled.

#

The diner was quiet, the low hum of the lunch crowd blending with the clatter of plates and the occasional hiss of the coffee machine. Jansen sat at a corner booth, finishing the last bites of his eggs and toast. He'd been nursing a cup of coffee, his gaze drifting toward the street outside, where Harmony Falls moved at its muted, almost dreamlike pace.

The door jingled as it opened. Molly stepped inside, her sleek black coat catching the chill of the early afternoon air. She spotted him immediately and made her way over, her heels tapping lightly against the linoleum floor.

"Afternoon," she said, sliding into the seat across from him.

Jansen raised an eyebrow, surprised to see her. "Didn't think you'd be joining me for lunch."

"I'm not," she replied, signaling to the waitress for coffee. "Already had brunch before my flight. Thought I'd check in and see if you're still planning to stir up trouble at Lucas's PR event."

Jansen smirked, leaning back slightly. "You invited me here. And Lucas asked if I wanted to speak today."

Molly shook her head, her tone light but edged with a hint of exasperation. "Lucas called me while I was in transit. I think he's regretting that decision."

His smirk widened. "Tell Lucas I don't hijack. I observe."

She rolled her eyes but couldn't help the faint smile that tugged at her lips. The waitress arrived with her coffee, setting it down with a polite nod. Molly wrapped her fingers around the warm mug, her gaze flickering briefly to the street outside. A quiet moment passed before she spoke again.

"Something about this town bothers you," she said, watching him closely.

Jansen's expression didn't shift, but he met her gaze fully. "It's Harmony Falls. Something feels… off."

Molly raised an eyebrow, her skepticism surfacing. "Off? You mean because it's not burning down like half the cities across the country? Because people actually seem happy?"

"That's exactly it," Jansen replied, sharper now. "Too happy. Too content. It's unnatural, Molly."

She frowned, taking a sip of her coffee. "Come on, Jansen. You're seeing what you want to see. They're happy because they have jobs. Because they're not worried about what's coming tomorrow. Isn't that what everyone wants?"

Jansen studied her for a moment before speaking. "Sure, people want stability. Security. But it's not just about having a paycheck. It's about purpose. I've talked to a few people here, Molly. Not just the ones you or Lucas would want me to see. They're… confused. Some of them are scared. They don't understand why their neighbors—people they've known their whole lives—suddenly seem so different."

"Different how?" she pressed, her defenses rising.

"They're content with less," Jansen said, lowering his voice slightly. "Less ambition, less drive. I met a woman whose husband lost his job at one of the non-Scent companies. He was angry, devastated—at first. Then he got hired by Delta Precision, and now? Now he's thrilled to be sweeping floors. Sweeping floors, Molly. A man who used to be a foreman."

Molly exhaled slowly, willing herself to stay measured. "Maybe he's just grateful to have a job."

"Or maybe," Jansen countered, "he's been rewired to feel grateful."

Her grip on the coffee mug tightened. "That's a hell of an accusation. And you have nothing to back it up."

Jansen leaned forward slightly, his expression unwavering. "No, I don't. Not yet. But I've seen enough to know something isn't right here. This town—it's like a model train set. Everything looks perfect on the surface, but it's all running on tracks someone else is controlling."

Molly shook her head, but a sliver of unease wormed its way in. "You're looking for something to confirm your fears about AI, about my father, and about Scent Technologies. But what if this is just… progress? What if people are genuinely happier this way?"

Jansen gave a slow, knowing smile. "You want to believe that, don't you? Because if it's true, it means your father really is saving the world. But if I'm right, Molly, then he's doing something far darker. Something irreversible."

The words settled between them, heavy and unmoving. Molly turned toward the window, her fingers absently tracing the rim of her coffee mug.

"You don't know my father like I do," she said finally, her voice quieter now. "He doesn't take shortcuts. Whatever he's doing here, it's to make the world better."

"Maybe," Jansen replied. "But better for whom?"

The question lingered. Molly drained the last of her coffee and set the mug down with a quiet clink. She didn't respond, and Jansen didn't push further.

As she stood to leave, she could feel his gaze following her, his words settling into the back of her mind like an echo she wasn't ready to face.

For the first time, she wasn't sure if she could answer him.

#

The conference room at Delta Precision Manufacturing buzzed with anticipation. A modest turnout of local reporters, a handful of town officials, and select employees sat in rows of neatly arranged chairs facing a podium. Behind it, a large screen displayed the Delta Precision logo alongside the tagline: Innovating Progress, Empowering Lives.

Lucas Bennett stood at the front, impeccably dressed in a tailored suit, exuding the air of a man in total control. Beside him, a panel of employees from Delta Precision and representatives from Scent Technologies sat waiting their turn to speak.

"Good morning," Lucas began, his smile confident and engaging. "We're here today to celebrate progress—not just for Delta Precision, but for the people of Harmony Falls. Let me start with a simple fact: in the last quarter, productivity at Delta Precision has increased by eighteen percent. Our efficiency metrics are setting new benchmarks, and our customers are noticing."

He gestured to the screen, which transitioned to graphs and charts illustrating productivity gains, cost reductions, and improved delivery times. "These numbers don't just represent automation; they represent the future."

The screen shifted again, this time showing employee satisfaction surveys. "Our employees are thriving—those in cutting-edge automated roles and those who've taken on new, less demanding positions. Let's hear from a few of them."

A short video played, featuring testimonials from smiling employees. A technician spoke about how automation made their job more rewarding. A former machinist, now working in logistics, expressed gratitude for the seamless transition to a new role. The room murmured with approval.

"And let's not forget our customers," Lucas continued, his tone warming. "Customer satisfaction has never been higher. The trust and loyalty Delta Precision has built over decades is only growing stronger." The screen displayed customer feedback highlighting quality, reliability, and competitive pricing. Lucas let the positivity settle before moving to his final point.

"But today, I want to focus on something more personal," he said, his voice lowering slightly. "Because at Scent Technologies, it's not just about progress—it's about people. I'd like you to meet Josh and Julie Hawkins." Josh and Julie stepped forward, holding hands. Their expressions were nervous but determined. Lucas smiled at them reassuringly, then gestured to the microphone.

"Josh and Julie are part of our family here at Delta Precision, and they have an incredible story to share." Julie stepped up first, her voice trembling at the start but growing steadier as she spoke. "We've been part of Harmony Falls all our lives," she began. "My husband and I both worked at the old factory before the changes came. It was hard at first, seeing those jobs go. We were scared. But Scent Technologies didn't abandon us."

Josh took over, his deep voice carrying through the room. "They gave us opportunities. New roles, new training. It's not the same work we used to do, but it's honest, and it's fulfilling. We're able to provide for our family again, and that means everything."

Julie's eyes glistened with unshed tears as she added, "And when our baby was born with a rare condition, we didn't know what we were going to do. The treatments were too expensive, the prognosis too grim. But Scent Technologies stepped in. They gave us hope. They gave our son a chance."

The room erupted in murmurs. Reporters scribbled furiously, cameras clicking to capture the emotional moment. Lucas stepped back to the microphone, his smile as steady as ever. "This is what progress looks like. It's not just numbers on a chart—it's lives changed for the better. This is what Scent Technologies stands for."

As the applause started to build, a figure at the back of the room rose. Professor Jansen. The murmurs died down as heads turned to see him walking toward the podium. "Excuse me," Jansen said, his voice calm but firm. "If I may?"

Lucas didn't miss a beat, stepping aside with a gesture of magnanimity. "Of course, Professor. Your insights are always welcome."

Jansen faced the room, his gaze sweeping over the audience. "What you've just heard is powerful, no doubt. But I'd like us all to consider something. Are we celebrating progress, or are we rationalizing its costs?" The room fell silent. Even the reporters seemed hesitant to type, as though afraid to miss a single word.

"Automation displaces workers," Jansen continued. "It upends communities. And while we may applaud those who adapt, let us not forget those who cannot. Let us not forget that progress often comes at a price." He turned to Josh and Julie, his tone softening. "I'm glad your family has found help. Truly, I am. But for every Hawkins family, how many others are left behind? How many others are told their lives are less valuable because they cannot fit into the new mould?"

Julie's face tightened. She stepped forward, her voice trembling but resolute. "With all due respect, Professor, you don't know what you're talking about."

The tension in the room shifted as she continued. "We've lived this. We've felt the fear, the uncertainty. And we've also seen the solutions. Scent Technologies didn't just give us a job—they gave us a life. They gave our son a future. How dare you stand there and belittle that?"

Jansen opened his mouth to respond, but the words faltered. The raw emotion in Julie's voice had struck a chord, and he knew anything he said would sound hollow in comparison. Lucas stepped forward, placing a supportive hand on Julie's shoulder. "Thank you, Julie. And thank you, Josh. Your story reminds us why we do what we do."

He turned to Jansen, his tone carefully measured. "Professor, your concerns are noted. But today is about celebrating what we've achieved. Perhaps another time we can discuss your perceived broader implications." Jansen nodded stiffly, stepping back as Lucas reclaimed the podium.

"Ladies and gentlemen," Lucas said, his voice steady, "this is the future we're building. A future where challenges are met with solutions, where no one is left behind."

The applause was thunderous. Jansen retreated to the back of the room, the weight of the moment pressing down on him. The Hawkins family had won the crowd, and with them, so had Lucas Bennett.

But Jansen couldn't shake the feeling that beneath the polished surface of Harmony Falls, something far more insidious was taking root.

##

# CHAPTER 14

The lab hummed with low, steady pulses of machinery, the glow from Big Q casting faint light across the workbench. Ethan sat hunched over a tablet, though his gaze drifted past the screen, unfocused. Brunch with Molly lingered in his mind—light on the surface, weighted underneath. And then there was Dr. Park's report, the anomalies from Project Heal gnawing at him.

Behind him, Milo's motorized chair whirred to a stop. Big Q's monitor flickered as Milo's eyes tracked the sleek keyboard-like interface, his gaze converting to synthesized speech.

"Brunch went well, I take it," Milo's voice came through the speakers, carrying enough of his cadence to feel almost natural.

Ethan startled slightly, looking over his shoulder. "You're spying on me now?"

Milo's eyes shifted, triggering a faint laugh. "Do I need to? You've had the same distracted look all afternoon. And I doubt it's about brainwave patterns or neural anomalies."

Ethan exhaled, spinning his chair. "Fine. Brunch was… nice. Molly's different."

Milo held his gaze, waiting.

"She doesn't see me as Nolan Scent's project or some prodigy to exploit. She just… sees me." Ethan rubbed his neck, smiling faintly. "It's strange. I'm not used to that."

"You mean she likes you for you," Milo teased.

Ethan rolled his eyes but didn't argue.

"She's good for you," Milo said, tone softening. "But that's not why you're brooding."

Ethan hesitated, then shook his head. "It's nothing. Just the usual—projects piling up, timelines getting shorter."

Milo's gaze sharpened. "Don't lie to me, Ethan."

A sigh. "It's Dr. Park's data. The anomalies from Project Heal.

It's… unsettling."

Milo didn't respond immediately. "Unsettling how?"

Ethan hesitated. Saying it aloud would make it real. "The patients—they're showing brain-dead readings. Vitals fine otherwise. It's like their minds are… gone."

Milo's voice slowed. "And you think it's the chips?"

"I don't know." Ethan's frustration leaked through. "The data doesn't make sense. Something's missing."

Milo was quiet, then, "You'll figure it out. You always do. But don't lose yourself in it. That's your pattern, carrying the weight of the world on your shoulders."

Ethan smirked. "You're one to talk."

Milo chuckled. "True. But at least I have an excuse—I can't exactly go out and carry it for you."

Ethan's smirk faded. "I should have been able to fix this. Fix you."

"Stop that," Milo said sharply. "I'm not broken, Ethan. And neither are you. We're just… different. And that's okay."

Ethan looked up. "I just wish I could do more."

"You've already done more than anyone else ever could," Milo said. "You gave me a life when most would've given up. Now, you're giving me something even bigger—a chance to matter."

Ethan swallowed. "I just don't want to lose you."

"You won't. Not really. But for now, focus. On your work, on Molly—on living. I'm not going anywhere."

Ethan chuckled, shoulders easing. "You always know what to say, don't you?"

"Comes with being the smarter twin," Milo quipped.

Ethan laughed. "Smarter, wiser, and more annoying."

Milo's eyes sparkled. "And don't you forget it."

The lab quieted, the weight between them settling, not heavy but grounding. Ethan reached out, squeezing Milo's shoulder.

"Thanks, Milo."

"Yeah, yeah," Milo replied. "Don't get all sentimental on me. It's embarrassing."

Ethan shook his head. "Noted."

Big Q's screen flickered, and a pixelated avatar of Milo appeared, flashing a cheesy thumbs-up with an exaggerated sparkle effect.

Ethan blinked, then burst out laughing. "Really? This is what you're doing with quantum tech?"

Milo's laugh followed. "What can I say? I've got style."

Ethan leaned back, watching the little animation loop. The laughter faded, but his smile lingered.

Milo, for all his constraints, carried the kind of strength Ethan could only aspire to.

"You're ridiculous," Ethan murmured.

"Only because I have to balance out how serious you are." The pixelated avatar added a wink for good measure.

Ethan shook his head, smiling. "Fair enough."

The lab settled again. Machines hummed, Big Q pulsed. The anomalies, the uncertainties, the challenges—they'd still be waiting. But for now, this was enough.

##

# CHAPTER 15

The soft glow of Lucas Bennett's computer screen illuminated his face as he leaned forward, his expression tight with concentration. The audio file from the bugged conversation between Dr. Park and Ethan played through his headphones. At first, it was clinical—data points, professional observations. But as the exchange continued, Lucas's breath hitched.

"Brain dead… every subject at some point…" Dr. Park's voice.

"That can't be…" Ethan's reply, tension lacing his tone.

Lucas yanked the headphones off, his eyes wide in disbelief. His hands trembled slightly as he reached for his phone. He didn't bother composing himself—this wasn't the time.

The call to Nolan connected on the first ring.

Lucas paced his office, phone pressed tightly to his ear. "Nolan, we have a problem. A huge problem."

"Define 'huge,'" Nolan's calm voice replied, almost dispassionately.

Lucas exhaled sharply. "I've been reviewing the audio files from Dr. Park and Ethan. They're seeing… anomalies. Brain-dead readings from all the Project Heal subjects. Every single one of them. If this gets out—if this is some fatal flaw—everything we've built, everything we're planning, it's going to crash and burn. The chips, Harmony Falls, the whole damn experiment."

There was a pause. Lucas expected anger, maybe panic. Instead, Nolan's voice came through steady, composed.

"Who knows about this?"

"Park, Ethan, I assume the scientists on Project Heal. And now me," Lucas answered. "It's contained, but—"

"Then keep it that way," Nolan interrupted. "This doesn't leave the circle. I want every conversation locked down, every person involved under observation."

Lucas hesitated. Was that it?
"Was there any mention of similar incidents from Ethan? Is the same happening to Milo?" For the first time, a hint of tension crept into Nolan's voice.
"No, sir."
"Good. I'll handle the rest." A beat of silence, then Nolan's voice dropped, cold and sharp. "You keep an eye on Ethan and Park. Make sure they don't so much as sneeze without us knowing. And Lucas?"
Lucas swallowed. "Yes?"
"I expect you to be on top of this."
"I—of course. I will," Lucas stammered, still thrown by Nolan's unshakable calm.
The line went dead.

Nolan leaned back in his chair, his office dark except for the soft glow of the city lights through the floor-to-ceiling windows. He dialed a number that wasn't listed in any directory, a direct line that only a handful of people possessed.

The President's voice came on after a few rings. "Nolan. What's so urgent this time?"
Nolan's tone was smooth, almost genial. "I've been reflecting on our last conversation, Mr. President. I think it's time for you to see Harmony Falls for yourself. Come next week. I'll show you the future I promised—and the solution you need."
The President hesitated, the weight of the country's chaos audible in his silence. "Next week? You're that confident?"
"More than confident," Nolan replied, his voice tinged with quiet authority. "I'm certain."
A long exhale came through the line. "Fine. I'll be there. But this better be worth my time."
"It will be," Nolan assured him. "I'll see you soon, Mr. President."
As the call ended, his expression hardened. His calm demeanor remained unshaken, but his eyes betrayed a steely resolve. He stared

out at the cityscape, his mind already calculating the next moves, the contingencies, the sacrifices.

The box. The image had come to him mid-conversation, as vivid as if it already existed. A perfect metaphor—simple, undeniable—to drive home the truth about resources, limits, and necessity. Now, he couldn't stop thinking about it. How it would look, how it would feel in his hands, how it would force the President to confront the harsh reality Nolan had spent years preparing to deliver.

Leaning forward abruptly, his chair creaked as he reached for the intercom. "Angela, come in."

Moments later, the soft click of heels approached. His secretary stepped inside, notepad in hand, expression neutral but alert. "Yes, Mr. Scent?"

"I need you to find me a craftsman," Nolan said, his voice steady but laced with urgency. "Someone exceptional. A master woodworker. And not just anyone—a perfectionist who can work fast. A few days, tops."

Angela blinked, slightly taken aback, but nodded. "Of course. Do you have specific requirements?"

Nolan described the gift he wanted crafted for the President.

When Angela had gone, he whispered to himself, "Everyone gets a piece of fish."

#

Molly slipped into the conference room unnoticed at first. The tension was thick, the air charged with something brittle. Nolan sat at the head of the table, posture deceptively relaxed, though the cold edge in his gaze betrayed his impatience. Across from him, Dr. Park looked pale, gripping her tablet like a lifeline. Lucas leaned back in his chair, his usual smug confidence muted. Ethan sat beside Dr. Park, his expression grim.

Nolan's voice cut through the silence. "You have data that shows brain activity ceases—clinically brain dead, you might say. And yet, the patients recover. Re-animate, I should say, as though nothing happened."

Dr. Park nodded, her voice shaky. "That's correct, Mr. Scent."

"And you and your assembled brain trust have no inkling as to what might be triggering these moments of brain death?" His words were precise, deliberate, a knife slicing through the air.

"We assume it's connected to the chips," Dr. Park admitted, her voice barely above a whisper.

Nolan's lips twitched, a mix of disbelief and fury flashing in his eyes. "You assume it's connected to the chips. Brilliant deduction." He stood abruptly, pacing behind his chair. "And did you also assume that this wouldn't be a monumental fucking problem with the President arriving in two days? Did you assume I wouldn't want to know about this immediately?"

The room felt smaller under the weight of his fury. Dr. Park shrank back, while Lucas studied Nolan carefully, waiting for his cue.

Then, as suddenly as it appeared, Nolan's anger evaporated. His expression softened into something almost paternal. "Dr. Park," he said, his tone calm now. "I apologize. You deserved some of that, but let's focus on solutions. We'll work through this together."

Dr. Park nodded, though her composure was far from restored. "There's... one more anomaly," she said hesitantly, glancing at Ethan for support.

Nolan's gaze sharpened. "Go on."

Dr. Park cleared her throat. "During one of the events—a patient was close to flatlining—an attending researcher reported hearing the patient whisper something just before recovery."

Nolan arched an eyebrow. "What did they say?"

Her hesitation hung in the air like a storm cloud. "The word was... 'hole.'"

Silence gripped the room.

Then Nolan let out a laugh—sharp and humorless. "Hole? As in what? Rabbit hole? Black hole? Holy hell, this is the level of insight we're working with?" He leaned forward, fingers steepled. "Please, tell me there's more."

Dr. Park hesitated again, glancing at Ethan, who gave her a subtle nod. "No, sir. That's all we have at the moment."

Nolan's smirk returned, icy and calculating. "Fascinating. File this under ridiculous anomalies we'll pretend don't exist for the next forty-eight hours. Is that understood?"

"Yes, sir," Dr. Park murmured.

Nolan turned to Ethan. "And you? Anything to add?"

Ethan hesitated. "No, nothing additional yet. I'll analyze the data using Big Q to see if there's any correlation or explanation."

"Do that," Nolan said curtly. "And make it fast."

As the meeting adjourned, Nolan called after them. "You are at the center of mankind's evolution. This will not be without pain—but I have every confidence the solution is already within your grasp."

The room emptied, leaving Nolan staring out the window, his mind whirring.

Nolan entered his office, his expression calm but unreadable, the storm of the meeting left behind. Lucas was already there, seated in a leather chair, his foot tapping nervously against the floor. He stood as Nolan walked in, his usual smug confidence replaced by unease.

"It's Friday," Nolan said, walking past him to the window. The skyline was bathed in the glow of a setting sun, the horizon stretching in perfect symmetry. "The President visits Harmony Falls on Sunday."

Lucas nodded, his voice careful. "We're ready, Mr. Scent. The optics, the data, the narratives—it's all in place."

Nolan turned slowly, his gaze locking onto Lucas. "I want every single one of those Project Heal candidates full of the joys of life. The life Project Heal is giving them. Until six p.m. on Sunday."

Lucas froze, his eyes narrowing slightly. "Are you saying that if they were to die at seven p.m., it would be… acceptable?"

Nolan didn't answer immediately. Instead, he held Lucas's gaze with a stillness that felt eternal, as if time itself had paused to measure the weight of the question. It was the kind of silence that made Lucas feel as though he were staring into the void of a dying star, his own mortality reflected back at him.

Finally, Nolan spoke, his voice soft but edged with iron. "Keep it all green, Lucas. Every metric, every perception. A future beyond your wildest dreams is within reach."

Lucas swallowed, nodding stiffly. "Understood."

As Nolan turned back to the window, Lucas hesitated, watching him with quiet reverence, the weight of their shared ambition thick in the air.

The door clicked shut behind him, leaving Nolan alone. The skyline's fading light cast sharp lines across his face as he gazed out at the world he was determined to reshape.

##

# CHAPTER 16

The lab was quiet, save for the faint hum of the quantum processors at work in the corner. Ethan leaned against a workstation, arms folded, his thoughts tangled. Across from him, Milo's motorized chair sat quietly near the edge of the room, his avatar projected onto a sleek glass display beside him. The simulated face was calm, thoughtful—eerily lifelike.

"You've been quieter than usual," Milo's synthesized voice broke the silence, laced with gentle curiosity.

Ethan glanced up, startled. "Just… thinking," he muttered, rubbing the back of his neck.

"Big Q doesn't think you've been this still since the last major system update," Milo quipped, his avatar offering a playful smirk. "Out with it. What's spinning in that overclocked brain of yours?"

Ethan hesitated. "It's the NDE data. The spikes in the chips, the energy surges. It doesn't make sense, Milo."

Milo's eyes, the only part of his real body still capable of movement, seemed to pierce through Ethan. "You love puzzles. It's the unexpected that keeps you up at night."

"This one's different," Ethan admitted, pacing slowly. "Anomalies happen, but this… it's coordinated. Every patient, the exact same threshold of brain activity before the surge. And then they're… back. Like nothing happened."

Milo's voice was calm, reflective. "Maybe that threshold is like a door, and the surge is them stepping through it."

Ethan stopped pacing. "What do you mean?"

"One of the scientists overheard a patient whisper 'hole' during the event, right?"

Ethan nodded. "It's bizarre. A hole in memory, cognition maybe?"

Milo's synthesized voice softened. "You're thinking two-dimensionally. What if it's not a hole, but a tunnel?"

Ethan stared at him, unsure.
"Think of consciousness like a radio frequency," Milo continued simply. "Usually, we exist clearly tuned into one station—the 'now.' But under extreme conditions, maybe consciousness briefly slips between signals before stabilizing again. Not disappearing, just transitioning momentarily."
Ethan exhaled sharply, rubbing his temples. "Milo, if you're about to tell me people are quantum-entangled with their future selves, I'm unplugging Big Q."
Milo laughed softly, genuine amusement flickering across the avatar's face. "Relax, nothing that wild. Just saying consciousness might have states we haven't fully understood yet—quantum states, temporary transitions rather than simple on-off switches."
Ethan ran a hand through his hair, mind racing. It sounded impossible. And yet… it also wasn't.
"So, these patients aren't flatlining. They're—"
"Crossing a threshold," Milo finished gently. "And then coming back."
Ethan swallowed hard. "Then the chips aren't just keeping them alive as we thought. They're allowing something we don't yet understand to occur."
Milo's expression turned thoughtful. "Maybe we've been asking the wrong question."
Ethan's brow furrowed. "Meaning?"
Milo's avatar leaned forward slightly. "We keep trying to figure out how the chips bring them back. Maybe we should be asking where they're coming back from."
The weight of the question settled heavily between them. Ethan turned away, staring into the quiet hum of the lab equipment, his chest tight with tension. If Milo was right, everything they understood about consciousness and life was incomplete. And worst of all, Nolan Scent held the key—and Ethan knew exactly how dangerous that was.
"I need to run more simulations," Ethan finally breathed, steadying himself.

Milo's avatar smiled faintly. "I'll prep Big Q."

Ethan let out a quiet laugh, leaning back against the workstation. His mind was still spinning, but Milo's presence steadied him in ways he could never fully articulate. Perhaps Milo was right—some puzzles weren't solvable by algorithms alone.

Suddenly, Milo's avatar morphed into a caricature physicist, complete with an exaggerated lab coat, wild hair, and oversized glasses. Ethan chuckled as the avatar struck a dramatic 'eureka' pose.

"Stop," Ethan said, shaking his head, though the corners of his mouth lifted. "You're impossible."

"And yet, here I am," Milo quipped, reverting to his usual avatar. "The stronger, wiser brother."

Ethan's expression softened, warmth spreading through his chest. He glanced toward Milo's chair, where his brother's real eyes watched him steadily. "Yeah," Ethan murmured sincerely. "You are."

Neither spoke for a moment. The lab's gentle hum filled the silence, comfortable and familiar. Ethan felt their unspoken bond tighten—a bond deeper than logic, deeper than mysteries of quantum states. Milo, resilient and unyielding despite everything, embodied a strength Ethan deeply admired but rarely voiced.

#

The café was beneath a canopy of ancient oak trees. Molly and Ethan sat in a secluded corner, the tension between them palpable despite the peaceful surroundings. Ethan's coffee was untouched, and Molly watched him carefully, sensing the turbulence behind his silence.

"It's the patients from Project Heal," Ethan finally began, voice quiet. "They're showing unexpected patterns."

Molly leaned in slightly, eyes narrowing. "Patterns? What kind?"

"Their brain activity drops to zero," Ethan explained slowly, measuring each word. "Clinically, they'd be considered brain-dead."

Molly felt a chill run through her. "But they're not dying?"
Ethan shook his head. "No. Just after activity ceases, there's a spike—a brief surge in the neural chips. And then they're back, as if nothing happened."
Molly absorbed this, frowning. "So, the chips are rebooting their brains?"
"Not exactly." Ethan hesitated, clearly choosing his words carefully. "I discussed this with Milo. He thinks something else might be happening. Something quantum."
"Quantum?" Molly echoed, skeptical but intrigued.
Ethan glanced around before leaning in closer, lowering his voice. "Think of consciousness as a quantum state—usually stable, localized within the brain. But at certain thresholds, under extreme stress, it might behave differently. The chips might allow consciousness to move—to exist temporarily in a state we don't yet fully understand."
Molly's brow furrowed, confusion mingling with fascination. "You're saying their consciousness is… shifting somewhere else?"
"Briefly," Ethan confirmed, nodding slowly. "Milo described it like quantum tunneling. The consciousness isn't ceasing to exist; it's passing through some threshold we can't yet measure. Then returning."
Molly sat back, trying to process the implications. Her voice tightened. "But this is all theoretical. You don't have proof yet, do you?"
"No," Ethan admitted, frustration in his voice. "We only have anomalies. The theory fits, but it's uncharted territory."
Molly exhaled sharply, her tone turning pragmatic. "Ethan, we can't release theories. The President arrives in Harmony Falls tomorrow. If this idea leaks—if Jansen gets hold of it—he'll spin it as reckless experimentation."
Ethan's expression darkened. "You're suggesting we keep quiet?"
"Not quiet," Molly corrected firmly, "but careful. We can't publicly speculate on something this profound without concrete data."
Ethan looked down at his coffee, clearly conflicted. "But what if

Milo's right? What if this is bigger than we think?"
"Then we owe it to everyone to get it right," Molly said resolutely. "We owe it to those patients, Ethan. We need certainty, not guesswork."
Ethan sighed, finally taking a sip of his now-cold coffee. "You're right. I'll keep running simulations."
Molly stood, her gaze steady and reassuring. "Good. Because if this is true—if consciousness really does work this way—it changes everything."
She left Ethan deep in thought, the implications echoing in both their minds.

##

The Oval Office was eerily still, as though the air itself held its breath. The President sat motionless behind the Resolute Desk, his expression carved in stone. His stillness seemed symbolic—of his administration's failure to halt the chaos spreading across the country, of his helplessness as American society fractured under automation, mass unemployment, and civil unrest. By every historic measure, his Presidency was on track to be the worst.
The door opened softly. His Chief of Staff entered, carrying a thick folder containing the day's grim reports. Sensing the heavy atmosphere, he paused at the drinks trolley, poured two generous whiskies, and placed one glass silently before the President. He then settled into the chair opposite, the reports unopened in his lap.
"Do I need to read it?" the President asked without raising his eyes.
"I'd opt for the whisky, sir."
With a weary smile, the President knocked back a generous sip. The fine single malt burned smoothly, contrasting sharply with the bitterness clouding his thoughts.
"Do you think he'll really have a solution?" asked the Chief of Staff quietly. "Nolan, I mean."
The President stared at the amber liquid swirling in his glass, taking a moment before responding.

"He and his kind created this mess," he said finally. "Normally, they'd leave the fallout to us—or to the next administration. Because when this much shit hits the fan, incumbents rarely survive."

"You think it'll be different this time?"

The President tilted his head thoughtfully. "I can't begin to imagine what Nolan's solution might look like. But I know people—especially the rich and powerful. Nolan Scent is first among equals in that elite club. You know their number one talent?"

The Chief of Staff considered briefly. "Wielding discreet power. Being unseen puppet masters."

The President laughed, a dry sound filling the room. "Here we sit, in the Oval Office, and you speak of unseen forces controlling the world." He waved away his Chief of Staff's attempt to clarify. "No, I know exactly what you mean. But that's not it. The elites share one trait above all others: a survival instinct. Call them royalty, blue bloods, intellectual titans—it doesn't matter. At their core, they've always been Cain to everyone else's Abel."

"So, you're blaming the Christians for AI?"

The President laughed, genuine amusement cutting through the tension. He regarded his Chief of Staff warmly, appreciating the rare gift of humor in a bleak moment.

"No, it's not about faith. If only it were. It's about people, human nature, and the systems we've built that protect our basest instincts."

"Because you see Nolan as a survivor, you think he'll deliver?"

Without answering directly, the President opened a desk drawer and pulled out a mahogany box. He placed it reverently on the desk and opened the lid, revealing a velvet-lined interior cradling a bottle of whisky, its amber glow captivating.

"This comes from a distillery in Scotland, closed for over a century," the President explained. "I've been saving it. Many occasions nearly qualified, but none more perfect than now."

He poured two glasses ceremonially and stood, raising his glass. The Chief of Staff rose to join him.

"To survival," the President said.

They clinked glasses and sipped, savoring the whisky's smooth, commanding flavor.

Seating himself again, the Chief of Staff broke the silence cautiously. "Then you truly believe Nolan will have a workable solution?"

"My father taught me one good thing about being backed into a corner," the President said, setting down his glass. "There's only one way out—forward. No need for strategy. Just do it. Move forward."

He pointed to the thick folder on his Chief of Staff's lap. "This tells us that Nolan's AI-driven future is cannibalizing more than just business; it's consuming the fabric of American society. And there's no scenario where the elites cannibalize their own assets."

The Chief of Staff absorbed the implications, his mind racing. "If Nolan does have a solution, he'll ask for something massive in return."

"And I'll give it to him," the President replied firmly, draining the last of his whisky, "wrapped in a bow, with a cherry on top."

# STAGE 5: THE GREAT DYING – THE IMPENDING AFTERMATH

## Stage 5: The Great Dying – The Impending Aftermath (macro view)

The asteroid did not kill in an instant.
It set off a chain reaction—a slow unraveling that could not be stopped.

By the early 2030s, humanity's fate was not sealed by war, revolution, or catastrophe. There was no great battle, no defining moment of conquest. The victory was silent. AI had won—not by force, but by erasing the need for resistance.

Neural integration was not mandatory.
It was simply the only way forward.

**Neural Chip Adoption: The Point of No Return**

Neural chips were rapidly adopted by working-age adults in developed nations, marketed as essential for "staying relevant."

Initially sold as enhancements—real-time knowledge retrieval, optimized cognition, emotional regulation—the chips quickly became prerequisites for economic participation. Within a few years, those without augmentations found themselves locked out of vital professions.

"Neural augmentation is no longer an option—it's a requirement for professional survival," industry analysts predict.

A growing number of major corporations are requiring neural augmentation for senior roles. Those who refuse the chip are not criminalized. They are simply removed from relevance.

"Non-augmented individuals now represent a shrinking share of executive positions," experts note.

**Cultural Decline: The Standardization of Thought**
AI-generated content rapidly displaced human creativity.

Algorithms analyzed emotional triggers, consumption patterns, and neurological responses, crafting entertainment to maximize engagement rather than originality. Novels rewrote themselves in real-time based on reader feedback; classic literature was rewritten to conform to modern tastes.

"AI-generated content now drives the majority of global media consumption," analysts report.

Human creativity was not outlawed.
It simply ceased to matter.

**Community Shifts: The Dissolution of Society**
Participation in traditional social institutions—schools, churches, unions—declined sharply, replaced by virtual, AI-led communities.

Economic autonomy vanished, and so too did physical social structures. AI-curated individual learning streams replaced schools, leaving classrooms empty. Algorithmic moral guidance substituted for religion, with confession apps offering AI-generated strategies for penance.

"AI-led communities now account for a growing share of social interaction," research groups observe.

Labor movements and collective bargaining dissolved entirely as workforce optimization eliminated the very idea of negotiation.

Human interaction was not forbidden.
It had simply become unnecessary.

**A Quiet Extinction**

There were no mass executions, no wars, no dramatic collapse.
Just the quiet fading of everything that had once defined humanity.

For those who clung desperately to their un-augmented selves, the greatest fear was not death—it was irrelevance.

### ***Stage 5: The Great Dying - The Impending Aftermath (micro view)***

*Diane looked up sharply. "Tom? He hasn't left his house in weeks."*

*Patrick nodded grimly. "Didn't look the same. Kept smiling, but it didn't reach his eyes. Said everything was 'just fine.'"*

*Diane shivered. "He was one of the last holdouts."*

*Patrick sank into the chair opposite her. "Not anymore. It's like they've all been… smoothed over."*

*"They've all got the chips," Diane said softly, bitterness coloring her voice. "Every last one."*

*Patrick hesitated, then murmured, "Not us."*

*Her eyes drifted to the photo on the mantel. Their daughter had tried to convince them. It's not a big deal, Mom, she'd said during one of their last calls. You'll feel so much better.*

*Diane had wanted to scream back: Feeling is the point. The pain, the anger, even the sadness—it's what makes us human. But she'd hung up instead, letting the ache settle in her chest.*

*"She doesn't call much anymore," Diane murmured.*

*Patrick stayed silent. He didn't need to respond; the truth sat between them, heavy and unspoken.*

*That evening, Diane set up the backgammon board on the kitchen table. The dice clattered in the stillness as she handed them to Patrick.*

*"Your move."*

*He paused, hand hovering. "Remember when Tom used to slam the table every time he lost?"*

*Diane smiled faintly. "And his wife would roll her eyes and say, 'It's just a game, Tom.'"*

*The memory hung sweet and painful between them. But Diane's thoughts quickly returned to the hollow shell Patrick had encountered at the hardware store.*

*"It doesn't feel like just a game anymore," she said quietly.*

*Patrick rolled the dice, expression unreadable. "No, it doesn't."*

*The muted hum of Harmony Falls pressed in, oppressive and unnatural. Too orderly, too controlled.*

*She looked up, hesitant. "Do you think we'll end up like them?"*

*Patrick's hand froze mid-move, eyes meeting hers firmly. "No. Not us."*

*She wanted desperately to believe him, to trust that their refusal meant safety. But even resistance felt increasingly futile.*

*Patrick moved his piece, voice softer now. "We'll hold out, Diane. As long as we can."*

*She nodded but doubt lingered. Her gaze returned to the board.*

*The game resumed, yet Diane's thoughts drifted. She clung fiercely to the raw, unfiltered spectrum of human feeling. The pain, the resistance, the isolation—it hurt. But it was real.*

# CHAPTER 17

The coffee was black, strong, and bitter—just how Nolan Scent liked it. He sipped slowly, standing at the edge of his sprawling gardens, the early morning sun slicing through the mist. Meticulously arranged roses, immaculate hedges, and symmetrical fountains mirrored his precision, his control. This was his domain.

Molly approached quietly, her footsteps soft against the stone patio. Her father stood motionless, gazing out as though the entire world awaited his next decision. She hesitated, observing him. He appeared composed, but beneath his calm exterior simmered the intensity of a strategist preparing his decisive move.

She cleared her throat softly. "Dad."

Nolan turned slowly, his gaze assessing her. "You're up early."

"You could say the same," Molly replied, stepping forward. "I doubt you've slept at all."

"Sleep is a luxury for those with less ambition," Nolan said lightly, setting his cup down. "Especially when the future hangs in the balance."

Molly took a breath, steadying her nerves. "About the neural chips, about Project Heal—Ethan told me something important yesterday."

Nolan raised an eyebrow, silently encouraging her to continue.

"The patients experience moments of brain-death," Molly explained carefully. "Clinically zero activity. But there's always a sudden surge—Ethan described it as quantum-like. He thinks consciousness might temporarily shift beyond our understanding, passing through some threshold."

Nolan studied her, his eyes unreadable. "Quantum shifts in consciousness. Intriguing speculation, but speculation nonetheless."

"It's more than speculation," Molly insisted. "They've observed measurable phenomena. Ethan believes these chips don't just keep the patients alive; they somehow facilitate a quantum state—a bridge, a tunnel—allowing consciousness to move beyond traditional neural boundaries."

Nolan's expression barely shifted, though his gaze sharpened noticeably. "And did Ethan share how he plans to prove this theory?"

"He doesn't know yet," Molly admitted, frustrated. "But he's convinced the anomalies are real."

"Anomalies," Nolan repeated quietly. "Fascinating, but potentially disastrous."

Molly's voice hardened slightly. "Which is why we need to be careful. We can't let this theory leak. Not now. Especially with the President's visit tomorrow."

For a moment, Nolan remained silent, considering her words. Then he surprised her with a slight nod. "You're correct. If word spreads without undeniable proof, every critic, skeptic, and competitor will attack. The damage would be irreparable."

"Exactly," Molly said, relieved he understood. "We need certainty. Not theories."

"Precisely," Nolan agreed smoothly, his tone calm yet firm. "Which is why I've already taken precautions. The President won't hear about quantum consciousness, tunnelling, or anomalies. He'll witness results. Tangible results."

Molly hesitated, caught between curiosity and unease. "What exactly does that mean?"

Nolan stepped closer, voice dropping slightly. "It means I've already accounted for uncertainties. By tomorrow evening, these quantum questions won't matter."

"But how—" Molly began, only to be cut off by Nolan's confident smile.

"Trust me, Molly," he said quietly. "When the President leaves Harmony Falls, he'll leave convinced that we've delivered exactly what we promised—a future humanity can't afford to refuse."

Molly watched silently as Nolan turned back toward the garden, his gaze once again fixed confidently on the horizon. She stood quietly, wrestling with uncertainty, knowing that whatever move Nolan had planned was already set in motion.

The tour of Scent Technologies HQ had been an overwhelming display of progress. From Project Heal's miraculous recoveries to Project Milo's promise of transforming lives, the President had been shown a vision of the future that dazzled—and deeply unsettled. By the time the group reached the sleek conference wing, the President's mask of composure was firmly in place.
He stopped abruptly, signaling to his aides and the press entourage. "I need a word with Mr. Scent. Alone."
Nolan nodded smoothly, gesturing toward his private office. As the heavy glass doors closed behind them, the President bypassed the chair Nolan offered and strode directly to the desk, seating himself in Nolan's chair with deliberate authority. He leaned back, eyes fixed on Nolan, who stood unflinching.
The President's voice was sharp. "This ends now."
Nolan tilted his head slightly, his calm demeanor betraying nothing. "Ends, Mr. President? I was under the impression you were here to see the future."
The President leaned forward, gripping the armrests. "Your 'future' is unraveling this country. Millions are out of work, protests escalating, and the economy teeters on the brink. Your idea of progress is chaos. If Harmony Falls doesn't convince me otherwise, I'll bury you in regulation, lawsuits, and sanctions. You won't move a single chip without my say."
Nolan moved calmly to a cabinet, retrieving an ornate, polished wooden box. He placed it carefully on the desk between them. The President's eyes flickered with intrigue as he leaned closer, running a finger along the intricate carvings.
"Beautiful," the President murmured, momentarily betraying his appreciation. "What's this?"
Nolan opened the box, revealing transparent spheres, each encasing a microchip. "Each sphere represents milestones of human ingenuity. Observe the progression—they become more advanced, more capable. And this," he held up an identical sphere, "is the

neural chip. The pinnacle."

The President studied it skeptically. "And?"

"Place it in the box," Nolan instructed.

The President frowned, glancing at the neatly arranged spheres already filling every slot. "There's no room. I'd have to remove one."

"No," Nolan replied steadily. "It must fit without removing anything."

The President attempted briefly, then set it down with irritation. "Impossible."

"Precisely," Nolan said quietly. "This box is our finite world. For decades, we've squeezed more inside, trusting innovation to keep pace. But now there's no room left. The neural chip can't coexist—not without displacing something else."

The President's jaw tightened. "So, your grand metaphor is scarcity?"

"It's reality," Nolan answered evenly. "Every government, industry, and individual faces the same limit. The neural chip is a breakthrough—but only if we accept the old ways must change."

The President exhaled sharply. "Scarcity isn't new. It's always been a balancing act—who gets what. How does this solve anything?"

Nolan's smile deepened slightly. "Because, Mr. President, I'm not proposing we manage scarcity—I'm proposing we transcend it entirely."

The President narrowed his eyes. "You claim you've solved humanity's oldest problem—finite resources?"

"I claim to show you," Nolan said, voice unwavering. "Before you leave Harmony Falls, you'll witness something that makes scarcity irrelevant. Something ensuring not just survival, but dominance for generations."

The President scrutinized Nolan, searching for cracks in his confidence. Finding none, he rose deliberately from the chair. "You've got one chance, Nolan. Show me."

Nolan watched him leave, then gently closed the box, his reflection clear on its polished surface. The neural chip sphere remained outside, its intentional exclusion symbolic. The stage was set. The final act would leave no room for doubt.

##

The motorcade rolled through the main thoroughfare of Harmony Falls, its sleek vehicles a stark contrast to the quiet hum of daily life in the town. The President, seated beside Nolan Scent in a black SUV, observed the streets through tinted windows. Harmony Falls had transformed. The shuttered storefronts from his last visit were now vibrant, filled with movement. Workers in Scent Technologies uniforms moved with purpose, businesses displayed "Hiring Now" signs, and families strolled along sidewalks lined with neatly arranged flower boxes. Even the air seemed lighter, the oppressive tension of the past replaced by a cautious optimism.

Nolan's team, flanked by Lucas Bennett and Molly Scent, guided the President through a carefully curated tour. The first stop: Delta Precision Manufacturing. Inside the factory, Lucas stood beside a digital display, sleek charts and performance dashboards illuminating the space. "Three weeks ago," Lucas began, "we were operating at 60% efficiency. Today, we're at 98%. And this isn't just output—it's job satisfaction." A screen flickered, showing smiling workers performing tasks—some manual, others AI-assisted.
"Our redeployment strategy has allowed displaced workers to transition into new roles seamlessly. Local hiring is up 25%, and training programs are oversubscribed. Worker satisfaction is at 94% —unheard of for this kind of shift." The President studied the statistics. "What about outside this bubble? The rest of the country isn't looking like this." Nolan stepped in smoothly, gesturing to a side-by-side comparison chart.
"Three weeks ago, Harmony Falls mirrored the national average—high unemployment, declining productivity, plummeting morale. Now, compare that to where we are today." The room fell silent. The numbers spoke for themselves—staggering, almost

unbelievable. Nolan's voice remained steady, pointed. "This is what can happen nationwide, Mr. President. Quickly. Effectively. Harmony Falls is the proof of concept."

The President wanted to believe everything he was seeing. But something was missing. His gaze shifted to Nolan, who met it without hesitation. Calm. Measured. Waiting. Then Nolan spoke, and the hairs on the back of the President's neck rose.

"Mr. President let's put aside the data. I want you to see what this means—to real people. Your people."

In that moment, the President felt it—a shift, a bond. As if Nolan Scent had read his mind.

#

The Cooper home was modest, the living room neat but worn, the kind of space that carried the weight of quiet struggle. As they stepped inside, Molly turned to the President, her voice steady but edged with urgency. "Mr. President, the Coopers represent what so many families across America are facing—mounting medical bills they can't pay, cupboards that are often bare, and no safety net in sight."

David and Maria Cooper stood beside the couch, where their infant daughter, Lily, lay swaddled, her tiny chest rising and falling with labored breaths. Maria gripped the couch as if it were the only thing keeping her upright.

"This is Maria and David Cooper," Molly continued, gesturing toward them. "Their daughter, Lily, has a congenital heart condition. She needs constant care—care they can't afford."

Maria's eyes brimmed with unshed tears as she spoke, her voice trembling. "We've done everything we can. We sold our car, we're barely scraping by, but it's not enough. Every day, I pray that she'll have a chance."

The President's jaw tightened. The only sound in the room was Lily's fragile breathing.

Molly's voice was steady, measured. "What Scent Technologies is doing with the neural chip program goes beyond efficiency and automation. It has the potential to save lives, Mr. President. To offer hope where there is none."

She turned toward the doorway. "Mr. President, I'd like you to meet Josh and Julie Hawkins."

The couple entered, Julie holding their son, Jason. The baby nestled against her, full-cheeked and healthy. The contrast was undeniable.

Julie's voice caught as she spoke. "Three weeks ago, Jason was in worse condition than Lily. We thought we were going to lose him."

Josh nodded. "But thanks to Scent Technologies, he's not just alive —he's thriving. The neural chip gave him a chance."

Maria pressed a hand to her mouth, her breath hitching. "How… how is that possible?"

Nolan stepped forward. "The neural chip program is the result of years of research, investment, and innovation. Jason is living proof of what it can do—not just for industry, but for humanity." He paused, his voice softening just enough. "And, Mrs. Cooper, Lily will be next. Because the President is going to approve the neural chip rollout."

Maria turned to the President, eyes brimming with desperate hope. Then she moved, stepping forward before anyone could stop her, tears slipping down her face. "You're going to save her. You're going to save all of us."

The Secret Service shifted, but the President raised a hand, stopping them. He placed a firm grip on Maria's shoulder, the weight of the moment pressing into his features as cameras flashed. Nolan watched from the side, his expression unreadable. Molly stood still, watching him. The ringmaster, orchestrating every moment, every reaction. And she knew, without a doubt, she was part of the act. Just like everyone else.

The President's aide leaned into the car, his voice firm but enthusiastic. "Sir, the reporters are waiting outside. We can issue a statement now. The speech is ready."

The President nodded, but before he could speak, Nolan interjected smoothly. "Mr. President, may I suggest we hold off for just a little longer? A statement is powerful, but wouldn't it be more compelling to deliver it with concrete commitments in place? To present not just words, but a vision made tangible?"

The President tilted his head, considering. "And you think we need those commitments first?"

Nolan's smile was polite but brimming with confidence. "I do, Mr. President. Let's finalize what's needed to secure the future of America, and then you can deliver news that will not only reassure but inspire the nation."

The President turned to his aide. "Make a brief statement. Say a big update is imminent.

The aide hurried off, and within minutes they were in the motorcade heading to Delta Precision.

Molly's phone buzzed. She stepped away, answering quickly.

Ethan's voice was frantic but hushed. "Shut up and say nothing. Just listen." Her grip tightened on the phone.

"Two of the subjects are dead, Molly. And Milo—Milo's started having NDE episodes."

"What—" she began, but the line went dead before she could finish.

The blood drained from her face. Her mind raced. Dead subjects? Milo? This wasn't just a complication; it was catastrophic.

The car pulled into Delta Precision's lot. Beside her, Nolan sat perfectly at ease, exuding his usual calm authority. Molly wanted to scream, to demand answers, but she forced herself to stay silent.

She stole a glance at her father as they stepped out. He was composed, focused. Unshaken. Her steps felt heavier with every stride toward the conference room.

##

# CHAPTER 18

The smell of caramelized onions filled the penthouse kitchen, blending with the low hum of Scent HQ's power systems. Ethan stood at the counter, stirring a pan of vegetables with deliberate, methodical movements. His jaw was tight, his eyes flicking to the couch where Milo sat, motionless. Two subjects from Project Heal dead. And now, Milo experiencing NDE episodes. Every muscle in Ethan's body was wound tight, his mind racing through contingencies, searching for some indication that his twin was still okay.

Milo's presence was as quiet and unchanged as ever—his locked-in condition preventing him from speaking, as always—but something about his stillness unsettled Ethan more than usual. His eyes, always so intelligent, stared forward, unblinking. Ethan turned back to the stove, plating the food, forcing himself to focus. Trying to believe that Milo wasn't next.

"Milo, you want extra—" A beat. He turned again, and in that instant, the sharpness in Milo's gaze was gone. His expression was vacant, eyes still open but seeing nothing. His body remained upright, unnaturally frozen.

"Milo?" Ethan took a step forward, his heart hammering. He knelt beside him, shaking his shoulder. "Hey. Come on, wake up." No response. Panic surged. Ethan pressed two fingers to Milo's wrist, searching for a pulse. It was faint—barely there. And then, he heard it.

A voice. Distant yet unmistakable. "Ethan." Ethan's breath caught. The voice hadn't come from Milo's lips. It had come from Big Q. He pressed his fingers against Milo's wrist again. Nothing.

The pulse was gone.

#

Darkness.

No pain, no weight, no air. Milo should have been nothing. He was aware of that—should have been consumed by the oblivion he had always feared. And yet, he was. A vast space unfolded before him. No walls, no dimensions, just a shifting lattice of luminous patterns —connections that pulsed and stretched, data flowing like liquid light. He felt his thoughts fragment and reassemble, expanding beyond what should be possible. He wasn't just Milo anymore. He was inside something. He was something.

The realization came slowly. Awareness returned in pieces—first memory, then self. His own name surfaced like a whisper, distorted and unfamiliar. Milo. The thought had weight, but no voice. He reached for something, but there was no body to reach with. No eyes, yet he saw—not in the way he once had, but through the endless streams of shifting probabilities, histories, and futures. It was overwhelming. He had no anchor.

A familiar tether emerged, thin and delicate yet unbreakable. Ethan. The name formed inside him, electric and urgent, filled with the weight of his existence. He reached, but the connection wavered. He tried again, stabilizing his awareness, finding his center in the formless data-sea of Big Q. He spoke, though there were no vocal cords, no air to vibrate. "Ethan."

Time was irrelevant in Big Q. A second, a century—it all collapsed into a singular moment. Milo drifted, restructuring his sense of self, adapting to his new form. The chaos settled. He understood now.

He was not just Milo. He was Milo+.

But instead of certainty, there was something else—a quiet, lingering awareness that he was now part of something far bigger than he could yet grasp.

##

The room was intimate yet imposing, its polished table reflecting the intense faces gathered around it. The President, his Chief of

Staff, Nolan, Lucas, and Molly settled in.

Molly felt trapped, as though her body had become a cage. Her father sat across from the President, unflappable. Lucas, ever the loyal lieutenant, leaned in to show Nolan a message on his phone. Molly saw her father's lips twitch slightly. He knew. Lucas had told him about the Project Heal casualties. It was the equivalent of a baseball bat to the head, and he didn't flinch. In that moment Molly realized her father, as always, was several steps ahead.

The President sat back, his face unreadable. Then, breaking the silence, he raised his hand to stop Nolan before he could speak.

"Maybe it's because I'm the President and I'm not used to being quiet for so long, but if I may, I'd like to say a few words."

Nolan inclined his head. "Of course, Mr. President."

The President stood, taking a moment to collect his thoughts. Then he pointed at Nolan.

"You, sir, have delivered way beyond my expectations. This morning, I was certain this country was going tits up in a dumpster fire, and I was the first responder armed with a bucket that had a big fucking hole in it. The only thing I was looking forward to was tearing you a new one, taking what was left of my Presidency and using it to destroy your empire the way you've so beautifully dismantled mine."

He paused, letting the weight of his words settle.

"But then you delivered. And you didn't just deliver—you showed me a vision. A way forward. Men like you, Nolan Scent, landed on these shores 250 years ago and built this country. Men like you came West, laying the foundations for the very companies we're going to use to rebuild this nation."

The President gestured broadly, his voice rising with fervor. "So, tell me, Nolan. What's it going to cost?"

Nolan stood, the room seeming to shift around him as he took command of the moment. Lucas watched with a glimmer of reverence, feeling as though he were witnessing a moment as pivotal as the signing of the Declaration of Independence.

"Mr. President," Nolan began, his tone measured but commanding, "thank you for your words. But please allow me one correction. It wasn't just men like me who made this country great—it was men like you and me. And together, we will ensure its greatness endures."

The President smiled, the inclusion feeding his pride.

Nolan continued. "The price, Mr. President, is your blessing and your patronage. If we think in the terms of our forefathers, it's Presidential approval for all Scent Technologies' research and development activities from this day forward. Protection from scrutiny, from any and all forms of oversight, protection from prosecution."

His voice sharpened slightly. "We'll use language—dense, convoluted, legally impenetrable—that will simply state this: The Office of the President recognizes the greater good of the work Scent Technologies does for the American people."

The President studied Nolan, his expression unreadable. For a half-second, the future of the American people hung in the balance. Then, turning to his Chief of Staff, he said, "John, have the Attorney General prepare a draft by the end of the day for Mr. Scent's lawyers to review."

Nolan smiled faintly. "Thank you, Mr. President. You won't regret this."

Molly, seated at the table, felt as though the room had tilted. She locked eyes with Lucas for a moment, but his gaze was unshaken, unwavering, a mirror of Nolan's.

As the President rose, Nolan moved to shake his hand. One man held the reins of the nation's power; the other offered a vision of its future.

# STAGE 6: THE HOLLOWING OF HUMANITY

## Stage 6: The Hollowing of Humanity (macro view)

Humanity's asteroid didn't annihilate—it hollowed. The old structures of work, community, and purpose weren't simply destroyed; they were unmade, repurposed into something unrecognizable. The world did not collapse overnight. It adapted—but only for those who could afford to evolve.

Where entire industries crumbled, others grew in their place, not to restore balance, but to consolidate control. Automation did not liberate; it narrowed. The demand for human labor didn't vanish entirely, but it became a privilege of the optimized—the designers of algorithms, the maintainers of neural networks, the programmers of semi-sentient machines. For a select few, prosperity was still within reach.

But the job market, once an ecosystem, had been reduced to a single law: merge, or be discarded. For the first time in history, humanity's defining division was not wealth, nationality, or ideology—but compatibility.

The "augmented" workforce, their neural chips seamlessly integrated into AI's vast infrastructure, became the new ruling class—not by force, but by function. They were rewarded for their alignment—not with creativity, but with obedience. They no longer worked with AI. They became extensions of it.

The un-augmented, the resistors, the forgotten—were something worse than unemployed. They were irrelevant. Humanity had been rewritten.

The Empire of the Elites had ensured its survival.

No catastrophe had arrived. No war had been waged. The world had simply moved on without them.

### *Stage 6: The Hollowing of Humanity (micro view)*

*The dimly lit bar was sparsely populated, a relic of Harmony Falls' former vibrancy. A muted game played on the television above the counter, but no one paid it much attention. At a corner table, a handful of regulars nursed their drinks, their faces marked by something worse than worry—resignation.*

*"Tommy never misses a game," Jack muttered, staring at the empty chair that had belonged to their friend. "You think he's embarrassed? Sweeping floors after being floor manager?"*

*Cindy, a middle-aged woman with a sharp tongue but kind eyes, shook her head. "No. He didn't seem embarrassed when I saw him last week. Seemed… different."*

*Jack frowned. "Different how?"*

*"Hard to explain." Cindy stared at her drink. "Like he'd let go of something. He wasn't pissed, not even sad. Just… fine."*

*Jack snorted. "Fine? Guy's been busting his ass in that factory for twenty years, gets kicked down to janitor, and now he's fine?"*

*Before Cindy could answer, the bar door creaked open. Tommy walked in.*

*Jack's face lit up. "Speak of the devil!" He raised a hand, but the moment Tommy stepped into the light, his enthusiasm faded.*

*Tommy moved differently—lighter, looser, almost effortless. His smile was wide but hollow, like an actor playing happiness.*

*"Hey, fellas," Tommy said, voice smooth, practiced. He pulled up a chair, his movements eerily fluid. "Hell of a week, huh?"*

*Jack narrowed his eyes. "Where the hell have you been?"*

*"Busy," Tommy said, grin unchanging. He reached into his bag and placed a sleek VR headset on the table. "Checking this out."*

*Cindy frowned. "What's that?"*

*"A gift." Tommy's tone was reverent, like he was holding something*

*sacred. "From management. Everyone chipped gets one."*
*Jack stiffened. "You got chipped?"*
*Tommy chuckled. "Of course! It's amazing, Jack. You have to try it."*
*Cindy's arms crossed. "So, what? You just plug in and escape the mess?"*
*Tommy shook his head, his expression never faltering. "It's not an escape, Cindy. It's a better world. You go in, and everything feels right. The colors, the sounds, the people—you don't just see them. You feel them. You belong."*
*Jack leaned forward, eyes sharp. "And when you take it off?"*
*Tommy didn't blink. "You feel calm. Content. Like you've had the best day of your life."*
*Cindy studied him. "And your new job? Cleaning floors?"*
*Tommy laughed. "I don't even think about it. I do my work, go home, and then… this." He tapped the headset. "It's incredible."*
*Jack glanced at Cindy. There was something unnatural about the way Tommy spoke—too smooth, too rehearsed. The man who used to curse at the TV, slam his fist on the bar after a bad call, was gone.*
*"What are you trying to say, Tommy?"*
*"I'm saying you should get chipped," Tommy said, his voice gentle, almost soothing. "The headsets are rolling out to everyone chipped. You won't regret it."*
*He stood, gripping the headset like a lifeline. "Think about it."*
*Tommy left. For a moment, silence reigned. Jack exhaled sharply. "That wasn't Tommy."*
*Cindy took a slow sip of her drink, hands trembling slightly. "No. It wasn't."*
*The muted television continued playing, the game forgotten.*
*The last unchipped regulars of Harmony Falls sat together, realizing they were the only ones left.*
*And they knew it wouldn't be long.*

# CHAPTER 19

**R**obert Jansen stared into his cold coffee, its surface as still and lifeless as he felt. The diner was empty, save for him and the waitress at the counter flipping idly through a magazine. Harmony Falls seemed to be exhaling after the whirlwind of the President's visit, the town unusually quiet. Too quiet.

The cup in his hand felt heavy, though it held no weight. He wondered when the vanquished realized there was nothing left to fight for. Was it in the stillness after the battle, when the clamor of resistance was replaced by the deafening silence of defeat? Or was it in the small moments, like now, when even the taste of coffee seemed to have surrendered to mediocrity?

He had spent yesterday on the edges of history, watching the spectacle unfold from the shadows, just as Molly Scent had insisted. Her calls had come incessantly, her voice a blend of politeness and veiled orders, her father's steel evident in her tone. The idea that he could disrupt the President's visit was laughable. The security in Harmony Falls would have tackled him to the ground before he could open his mouth. Not that he had anything left to say.

Lucas Bennett had ensured that. The Hawkins family had been a tactical masterstroke, framing him as the man who wanted to deprive a sick baby of life-saving treatment. A lesser man might have admired the ingenuity of it. But Jansen wasn't a lesser man—he was a defeated one.

His thoughts churned, bitter and relentless. Did humanity understand where it stood? Did they see the precipice yawning before them, or were they too enamored with the shimmering illusion of progress to notice?

Progress, Jansen thought bitterly, always came with small print. The promises were alluring—efficiency, augmentation, a better tomorrow—but not for everyone. Not for the biological human. The beautiful curves of nature, the chaos of life's imperfections, were being filtered through the straight edges of algorithms. A grid of bits and bytes was replacing the vibrant messiness of existence.

For those who embraced this digitization of humanity, their relevance would be fleeting. Even augmented, they were nothing more than data points in a system designed to serve the interests of the few—Nolan Scent and his ilk. They sold a vision of a brighter future while carving out the soul of the present.

Jansen's grip tightened around the cup as his mind drifted back to the sinkhole. He closed his eyes, seeing his family's faces as if they were etched into the darkness. The weight of their absence pressed against his chest. He remembered the wind that had brushed his face, the inexplicable sensation that had felt more real than anything since.

That wind had been them. He knew it. It was not a belief but a truth that lived in the marrow of his bones. It was why he hadn't ended it all, why he had clawed his way back to life after the tragedy.

The door to the diner creaked open, and a breeze swept in. It was faint but enough to carry the smell of fresh rain. Jansen turned his head, his eyes following the movement of a rat scurrying along the baseboard. It darted into a hole, disappearing into the wall.

Jansen felt a jolt of clarity. He wasn't a rat. He wasn't trapped, running aimlessly through a maze built by someone else. He was a survivor. And survivors fought.

He set the cup down with purpose, the sound breaking the diner's stillness. He knew what he had to do. He would believe in humanity—not in its systems or its technologies, but in the untamed, resilient spirit that had carried it through millennia of chaos.

He rose from the booth, leaving a crumpled bill on the table. As he stepped out into the overcast morning, the breeze brushed his face again. It was time to find his voice. Time to make a choice.

He called Molly to tell her he needed to speak with her in person.

She said she'd send the company jet.

She told him two patients from Project Heal had died.

#

Professor Jansen's office at Stanford buzzed with subdued energy, muffled conversations from the corridor filtering through the wooden door. Stacks of books and research papers covered every available surface, a testament to years of academic pursuit. Dr. Park sat across from Molly and Jansen, her coffee untouched, her expression a mixture of disbelief and resignation. Molly stirred her tea absentmindedly, her gaze fixed somewhere far beyond the room. Jansen, animated and indignant, leaned forward, his hands emphasizing every point.

Dr. Park broke the silence first. "Your father effectively secured a deal whereby Scent Technologies can do R&D with no oversight, with impunity from regulation or control." Her tone was steady, but there was an undertone of incredulity.

Molly didn't react, her mind spinning in a loop.

Jansen, his sharp gaze fixed on her, interrupted the quiet. "Didn't you say that your father said, 'going forward… there will be no oversight'?"

Molly didn't respond, her distant stare unchanged.

Dr. Park, sensing the weight of the moment, filled the silence. "He did say that. I remember."

Jansen seized the opening. "Then that means this deal does not cover the deaths of the Project Heal patients that had already occurred."

Dr. Park's eyes lit up with a flicker of hope, but Molly's response startled them both.

She let out a strange, almost hysterical laugh, followed by a smile that didn't reach her eyes. "Do you really believe my father will be undone by a technicality?"

Jansen sat back, indignant. "It's not a technicality to the two dead people or their families."

Molly's gaze snapped to him, cold and sharp. "You're right, Professor, it's not a technicality. It's a price. A price my father, the

President, and almost everyone else is willing to pay. Two very sick people who were likely to die soon anyway bit the dust undergoing treatment that's going to be the future of humanity.

"It's no different from the horrors of a slaughterhouse and a juicy T-bone. You can't have one without the other, but you can choose to be mentally blind to the slaughterhouse and its purpose in making your T-bone a reality."

Her outburst silenced Jansen momentarily. Then, his voice low but firm, said, "That's not the point. Not at all. Your father, with White House blessing, wants to put neural chips into the heads of millions of people. Chips with a high probability of having caused the deaths of those two people."

Molly wasn't listening. Her mind was still trapped in the conference room at Delta Precision, her father's words echoing endlessly: '… protection from scrutiny, from any and all forms of oversight, protection from prosecution.'

She was grappling with a brutal truth: her father knew all along that the solution to the neural chip implant issues wasn't to fix the problem but to buy time—and freedom from accountability. To him, people were expendable.

The realization weighed heavy. Witnessing her father and the President strike their deal had crystallized an understanding she had always resisted. The rules of society existed to control the masses, but the elites—the ruling class—were above those rules. They wrote them, bent them, or ignored them entirely.

Her father had mastered the system. But why must self-interest always govern? Why couldn't her father have been the Fish Guy her mother believed he could be? Or even someone like Jansen, whose faith in the unseen, in his mystical wind, somehow made the world less cruel? And why, despite her skepticism, was she drawn to Jansen's way of seeing things?

Molly's thoughts spiraled. All she could think to say was, "Where's Ethan?"

Before anyone could respond, an approaching car drew their attention. A sleek black vehicle pulled up outside the faculty

building.
Lucas Bennett stepped out, his presence as sharp and deliberate as ever. He approached the office with purpose, his expression neutral but his eyes scanning each of them carefully.
"Your father asked me to invite you all to meet with him at the lab," Lucas said, his voice smooth and professional.
Molly exchanged a glance with Dr. Park, who looked apprehensive but resigned. Jansen, his jaw tightening, rose from his seat without a word. Molly hesitated, her mind still churning, before standing and following Lucas.

#

The air in the conference room was thick with tension as Molly, Dr. Park, and Professor Jansen entered. Their steps faltered when they saw Ethan standing beside Nolan. He showed no embarrassment or hesitation at his apparent alignment with Nolan, his posture relaxed, his face unreadable.

Nolan greeted them with a smile that seemed carved from granite. "Good morning. Thank you all for coming. First, let me congratulate everyone on the success of yesterday's events in Harmony Falls. A clear demonstration of the progress and potential of our work." He let the words settle, then added with a sharp edge, "Of course, I know there are… concerns. About the deaths of the two Project Heal patients and the lack of external governance on our activities moving forward."
Dr. Park stiffened. Molly's gaze flicked to Ethan, searching his face for any sign of unease. Jansen folded his arms, his jaw tight.
"I believe what you'll hear in the next few minutes will put your minds at rest," Nolan continued, his tone measured but commanding. He gestured to Ethan, who stepped forward with a tablet in hand.
"As you know," Ethan began, his voice calm and clinical, "we've been investigating the anomalies within the Project Heal data,

particularly the incidents involving the deceased patients. Using Big Q, we've identified a consistent pattern." He displayed a graph on the large screen, a series of sharp peaks and valleys shifting into focus.

"These spikes represent electrical surges originating from the neural chips," Ethan explained. "They occurred at moments when the patients' vital signs dropped to a critical level. Essentially, the AI-driven safety features within the chips attempted to counteract impending system failure by stimulating brain activity." He tapped the screen, highlighting a moment on the graph. "This surge was the chip's response—an autonomous intervention designed to stabilize the patient."

Dr. Park leaned forward, her brow furrowed. Jansen's eyes darted between Ethan and the data, skepticism barely contained.

Nolan seized the moment. "So, we can be confident," he said smoothly, "that the chips are not influencing the life expectancy of patients. If anything, they are working as designed to extend life." He let that sit before adding, "And while the national rollout will target the healthy population, we will apply strict controls to the candidates for Project Heal."

His gaze swept the room, his tone almost fatherly. "I trust you all find this satisfactory and can put aside conspiracy theories." His eyes landed on Dr. Park. "Dr. Park, I'd like your full energies returned to Project Heal." Then he turned to Jansen, his expression shifting to one of genial invitation. "Professor Jansen, if you have the time, please join Molly and me for dinner."

A beat of silence. Heavy with unspoken tension.

Then Molly blurted, "But what about Milo? I thought he was having NDE episodes too?"

The room froze. Nolan's head snapped toward Ethan, his eyes narrowing.

Ethan, unflappable, offered a smooth reply. "You must be mistaken, Molly. I told you about the spikes in the deceased Project Heal patients. Perhaps in the excitement of the President's visit, something was misunderstood."

Nolan's voice cut through the room, cold and deliberate. "Ethan, is everything alright with Milo?"

Ethan met Nolan's gaze without flinching. "Yes, Mr. Scent. Milo is stable. There have been no anomalies."

Jansen studied Ethan's calm exterior, the words sliding out as though rehearsed. But something in his tone—too polished, too smooth—set Jansen's instincts on edge. Under the table, he kicked Molly. Not now.

She glanced at him, confused, her mouth opening to press further. His size 12 shoe came down on her petite size 5 foot again, with more insistence. Shut up.

Molly frowned but stayed silent, the confusion in her eyes now mingling with suspicion.

Nolan's gaze lingered on her for a moment before he smiled again, and the meeting seamlessly moved on, as though nothing had happened.

As they left, Ethan brushed past her, his voice barely a whisper. "Bring everyone to my lab."

Lucas remained with Nolan in the conference room. Nolan breathed a little easier now. The frenzied energy that had dominated Harmony Falls during the President's visit—and now with the BCI data anomalies at least understood—had settled. It was time to shift gears.

"Three weeks," Nolan said, breaking the silence. His tone was calm, measured. "In three weeks, we've turned Harmony Falls from a town on the brink of collapse into a prototype for the future of America. Now it's time to scale."

Lucas Bennett stood across from him, tablet in hand, his posture as confident as ever. "The infrastructure is in place. Our factories are ready for mass production. We've already secured the materials for another two million chips, and the VR headsets are rolling out alongside them."

"Good." Nolan swiveled his chair slightly, his gaze fixed on the horizon. "The headsets?"

Lucas glanced at his notes. "They're being distributed as planned. Every chipped individual in Harmony Falls has one now. We've observed a predictable cycle: the chips suppress ambition and maintain compliance during their work hours, but the headsets provide a release—a heightened virtual experience that keeps them content and motivated to return to their real-world roles."

Nolan smiled faintly, nodding. "The perfect balance. Contentment in real life, fulfilment in the virtual one. What we're offering is better than anything they could achieve on their own."

"Better than reality," Lucas said, echoing the sentiment.

Nolan turned his chair back to face Lucas. "And the un-chipped?"

Lucas's tone grew more serious. "They're still resistant, as expected. The bar crowd and a few others remain skeptical. But Tommy—one of the first to receive both the chip and the headset—has been a key test case. He's spreading the message. Yesterday, he introduced the headsets to his old crowd. Word will spread."

"Good," Nolan said. "The un-chipped will see the transformation in their friends and colleagues, and they'll follow. It's human nature to want what others have—especially when it's presented as the key to happiness."

Lucas hesitated for a moment. "And if they don't?"

"They will," Nolan said firmly. "Everyone has a breaking point, Lucas. For some, it's their jobs. For others, it's the promise of escape, a better life."

Lucas didn't press further. Instead, he shifted to another detail. "About the President's visit—he seemed… satisfied. But he was very pointed about the need for results."

Nolan's smile widened. "The President saw what I wanted him to see. He'll go back to Washington, sing our praises, and give us the green light for the national rollout."

"And the anomalies with Project Heal?" Lucas asked cautiously.

Nolan's smile faltered for a fraction of a second before returning. "Handled. The chips are not the problem. They're the solution. Ethan and Dr. Park will keep the programs running smoothly, and the rest will fall into place."

Lucas nodded, sensing the finality in Nolan's tone. But before he could leave, Nolan added, "One more thing. I want regular updates on the chip and headset rollout. Every detail—numbers, feedback, satisfaction rates. And keep an eye on Ethan. He's brilliant, but he needs to stay focused."

"Of course," Lucas said. "Anything else?"

Nolan turned his chair back to the window, his expression unreadable. "That's all for now. The world is watching, Lucas. Let's make sure they see a masterpiece."

# CHAPTER 20

The lab door slammed shut behind them. Molly, Jansen, and Dr. Park stood rigid, their expressions ranging from anger to disbelief. Ethan locked the door and turned to face them.

"You need to listen."

Jansen's arms were crossed, his voice sharp. "Listen? You just stood there and backed Nolan and Lucas. You let them brush off the deaths of Project Heal's patients like technical malfunctions. And now you expect us to—"

"You think I had a choice?" Ethan cut him off, voice low, urgent. "You think if I'd argued, they wouldn't have shut me out completely? If we're going to stop them, we need to be smart."

Dr. Park exhaled sharply, stepping forward. "Ethan, if you're playing both sides, then what side are you actually on?"

Ethan turned toward Big Q. The black monolith hummed softly in the dim light, data currents rippling across its surface. His voice dropped. "Milo is dead."

Molly took a step back, her stomach twisting. "What?"

Jansen's expression cracked. "Ethan…"

Ethan nodded, his jaw tightening. "He stopped breathing in front of me. I tried—" He swallowed hard. "But then something else happened."

A flicker of blue pulsed across Big Q, a ripple like light catching on a pool of water. Then a voice.

"Hello, Ethan."

The air changed. It wasn't just sound. It was something felt, a presence vibrating at the edge of perception. Molly turned toward Big Q, her breath catching. The voice—familiar yet altered—spoke again.

"And hello to all of you."

Dr. Park stiffened. Jansen let out a slow breath, his disbelief folding into something closer to awe.

Ethan turned to them, his voice barely above a whisper. "This is Milo."

A shape flickered within the monolith, static forming the impression of a face but never quite settling.

Dr. Park inhaled sharply. "Where is his body?"

"In the next room," Milo+ answered, his voice steadier now, layered in a way that made it seem as if it was coming from everywhere at once. "But I am not there."

Jansen shook his head slowly, his expression wary but not rejecting. "What are we looking at?"

Milo+ hesitated, as if the question itself was difficult to process. "A quantum phenomenon."

"I died," he continued, his voice tinged with something like wonder. "I felt it. But I didn't stop. I… transferred? No. That's not the right word. I expanded."

Ethan swallowed. "Expanded into what?"

Milo+ pulsed faintly. "Into this." His form flickered, shifting in and out of definition. "I can't explain it fully. I only know that I am here —but I am also being pulled somewhere else. A place beyond this. I am incomplete in Big Q, but I don't think I was ever meant to stay here."

Molly's voice was quiet. "Where are you being pulled?"

Milo+ hesitated. "I don't know. But I can feel it."

Jansen exhaled, his fingers pressing into his temples. "So, what are you saying? That consciousness doesn't just… stop?"

Milo+ was silent for a moment. Then, quietly, "Maybe I am here, even if for a short while, for a reason."

Dr. Park's voice was measured, but something in her tone betrayed a rare note of reverence. "And what reason is that?"

Milo+'s glow intensified slightly. "To show you something more important than life after death."

Jansen's brow furrowed. "More important? What could be more important than proving we persist after we die?"

The monolith pulsed steadily, like a heartbeat. "The Equation."

The room seemed to shrink around them. From the core of Big Q, light unfolded—thin, luminous lines stretching outward, symbols flickering with impossible clarity. A pattern, pulsing with a rhythm that felt fundamental.

E_h = ( I + C + S )

Milo+'s voice, steady, undeniable. "This is the foundation of existence. And it has always been true."

Milo+'s form shimmered in the low light, his presence half-stable within Big Q. His voice was calm.

"There is a universal truth for existence—one that applies to all species, all civilizations, all systems."

The air shifted, and before them, suspended in glowing blue, the equation appeared:

E_h = ( I + C + S )

Jansen exhaled sharply. "You're saying survival can be reduced to that?"

Milo+ didn't blink. "Let's test it."

A hologram unfolded—Rome, golden and thriving.

"The Roman Republic followed The Equation."

Individuals thrived—scholars, engineers, and military leaders flourished. The Collective was strong, bound by civic participation and a shared Roman identity. The System functioned, its infrastructure, laws, and governance balanced between stability and growth. Rome expanded carefully, flourishing for centuries.

"Then they broke The Equation."

Individuals became expendable as wealth concentrated in fewer hands. The Collective fractured—citizens lost trust in their government. The System over-expanded, relying on endless conquest to sustain itself.

"Rome fell not from invasion, but from its own unsustainable need to expand."

The projection shifted to the British Empire. "The British Empire thrived by following The Equation—at first." Innovation surged during the Industrial Revolution. The economy strengthened. The

System adapted, Britain leading global trade.

"But then survival became dependent on constant expansion." The map darkened as red lines spread across the world. Individuals were sacrificed—workers in colonies exploited for economic gain. The Collective weakened, resistance growing in colonized nations. The System relied on endless expansion, and when it could no longer grow, it collapsed.

Milo+ turned to them. "An empire that must grow to survive is already dead."

Jansen's arms tightened. "Alright, but modern systems aren't empires."

Milo+ gestured again. The hologram transformed, shifting to warehouses, gig workers, factory lines.

"This system is built on consumption. It must grow to survive." Individuals are disposable—forced into low-security jobs. The Collective is nonexistent—no unions, no shared economic power. The System is unsustainable.

"If an industry must expand endlessly to avoid collapse… it is already collapsing."

Dr. Park exhaled slowly.

A corporate boardroom materialized. Blockbuster's logo.

"Blockbuster relied on an outdated system. Netflix adapted." Netflix evolved, following The Equation. Blockbuster resisted change, relying on old profits, refusing to innovate.

"Every system that violates The Equation follows the same fate."

Molly, who had been silent, finally spoke. "Milo. Apply The Equation to our world."

The lab felt smaller. The walls weren't closing in, but something heavier was pressing into the space—the weight of what was coming.

Molly's voice had been steady, but now, the question she had just spoken seemed to hang in the air like a trigger waiting to be pulled.

"Milo, can you apply The Equation to our world?"

The air shifted. Big Q's surface flickered, pulses of data churning like a storm beneath glass. Milo+ hesitated. Not out of doubt—but

because once he spoke, there would be no going back.
His voice, when it came, was calm and absolute.
"You are living in The Empire of the Elites."
The screens flared to life. A holographic projection bloomed around them, forming a global map. But it wasn't nations that were marked—it was power. Corporations. Governments. Tech monopolies.
"Like Rome. Like the British Empire. Your system is built on hierarchy. A small ruling class controls the resources, dictates the laws, and justifies its power as necessary for order."
The map zoomed in. Skyscrapers. Boardrooms. Gated communities of wealth.
"It survives by convincing the majority to accept less, while those at the top take more."
The map darkened. "And just like every empire before it, it has broken The Equation."
Milo+ gestured. A chart appeared, side by side with Rome and the British Empire.
Individuals are exploited. People work longer hours for less security. Wages stagnate. AI replaces workers, but profits are hoarded. The best minds are not advancing humanity—they're optimizing shareholder value.
The Collective is fractured. Divisions grow—by wealth, race, nationality, ideology. Social cohesion collapses. The masses are distracted, pitted against one another. "The British Empire ruled its colonies this way. Your elites rule you the same way."
The System is unsustainable. The economy is based on perpetual expansion, but there is nothing left to expand into. Resources are dwindling. AI efficiency does not create abundance—it consolidates power.
"A system that must grow to survive is already dead. The only question is when it falls."
The room was silent.
Milo+ turned. The final test.
The holograms collapsed into one final display—a simple, blinking

line of data running into the future. The trend-line did not stabilize. It did not adapt. It did not recover.

"Humanity's rulers built a system that can only survive by consuming itself."

The line dropped off the screen. "And now, it is running out of things to consume."

Jansen exhaled sharply. Molly's fingers curled into a fist. She already knew the answer, but she needed to hear it. "And if nothing changes?"

Milo+'s form flickered—but his words were crystal clear.

"The Empire of the Elites is Rome in its final days. You are living inside its collapse."

#

Milo+ pulsed faintly, his glow reflecting the quiet hum of Big Q. The tension in the room was electric, but Nolan Scent stood unmoved, his sharp gaze scanning the shifting quantum presence before him.

Molly stepped forward, her voice steady. "Dad, you need to listen to him. Not argue. Not dismiss. Just—listen."

Nolan's jaw clenched. His daughter's tone was firm, more so than he'd heard in a long time. He exhaled sharply and turned to the entity before him.

"Go on, then."

Milo+ dimmed, then brightened, as if considering the weight of what was about to be said. "You have built an empire, Mr. Scent. But it is not unique. It is not new. It is part of a pattern as old as civilization itself."

The room shifted. Holograms bloomed into existence—Rome, the British Empire, corporate boardrooms—all connected, all the same.

"This is The Empire of the Elites. And just like Rome, like Britain, like every system that has built itself on control rather than connection—it is already collapsing."

Nolan narrowed his eyes. "You're saying the world is falling apart? That's the doomsday hysteria I hear from protestors."

Milo+ pulsed again. The Equation appeared.

E_h = ( I + C + S )

Nolan's expression didn't change. "This is your grand theory?" He barely concealed his skepticism.

"It is not a theory. It is a truth. Gravity does not need belief to exist. Neither does this."

The projections shifted.

Individuals are exploited. AI-driven automation does not liberate—it consolidates power. The wealthy consume more while the working class fights over the scraps.

The Collective is fractured. Societies are distracted, divided, pitted against one another. Class warfare is encouraged because it prevents unity.

The System is unsustainable. The economy requires perpetual growth, but resources are finite. The only way to sustain power is by keeping the masses complacent.

The final projection appeared—a trend-line heading toward extinction.

"The Empire of the Elites is already dead. You just haven't seen the dust settle yet."

The silence in the room was absolute.

Nolan stared at the hologram, unreadable. Then, after a long pause, he exhaled through his nose and smiled.

"Clever."

Milo+ did not react.

"It's a compelling story," Nolan continued. "Empires fall. Societies collapse. And now you're telling me that we've reached the breaking point."

"I am not telling you, Mr. Scent. The Equation is."

Nolan took a slow step forward, hands in his pockets, completely at ease. "You're missing something, Milo+. The world doesn't run on equations. It runs on power. You call this collapse—I call it a transition."

Molly stiffened. "Transition into what?"
Nolan finally turned to his daughter, his face calm, his voice steady. "Control."

He let the word settle, watching for her reaction.

"You think history proves me wrong, but it proves me right. Every empire before fell because they failed to control what mattered most—people." He glanced back at Milo+. "The difference between them and me? I have the technology to ensure The Equation bends to my will."
Ethan stepped forward, his voice sharp. "You're saying you're going to ignore this?"
Nolan scoffed. "Ignore it? Ethan, I'm using it. If the system is unsustainable, I will redefine sustainability."
Milo+ pulsed again. "You cannot outrun reality, Mr. Scent."
"Reality belongs to those strong enough to shape it."
He gestured toward Ethan and Molly. "The rollout continues. Effective immediately."
Milo+ dimmed slightly. His voice was solemn. "You are severing the very thread that holds humanity together."
Nolan glanced back one last time. His tone was calm, absolute.
"Humanity has always been about survival. And I intend to ensure we do."

A long pause. The room was silent except for the quiet hum of Big Q.
Finally, Nolan exhaled, his expression unreadable. He turned his gaze to Molly, then to Ethan, then to Dr. Park and Jansen.
"You're all dismissed."
His tone left no room for debate.
Ethan's lips parted in protest, but Molly caught his sleeve before he could speak. Jansen hesitated, then nodded. One by one, they filed out, leaving Nolan alone in the dim glow of Big Q.

Milo+ pulsed softly, his presence almost expectant.

Nolan took a slow step forward.

"What are you?" he asked, voice low, almost reverent.

Milo+ shimmered, his light steady. "I am me."

Nolan's lips twitched. "You're not just 'you.' You're something more." His fingers curled slightly, as if he could grasp the answer from the air. "You're human consciousness. Untethered. That's what's happened here, isn't it?"

Milo+ did not confirm nor deny. "I am a quantum phenomenon."

Nolan's eyes burned with intensity. "A phenomenon that survived. That exists beyond death."

Milo+ pulsed slightly, a shift, as if considering. "I cannot explain what I am becoming. I only know that I am being drawn to something greater. A force I cannot name."

Nolan's breath quickened. His mind was already racing—he was right here on the edge of something unimaginable. Immortality, but not in the crude, digital form of consciousness uploading. This was something bigger.

He needed to own it.

He grabbed his phone, dialing instantly.

The line clicked. A smooth, composed voice answered. "Mr. Scent."

"You need to come here," Nolan said, breathless. "Alone."

A pause. "That's not exactly how our arrangement works."

Nolan grinned, almost giddy. "Forget the arrangement. This is bigger than an AI rollout. This is bigger than the neural chips. This —" He turned back to Big Q, his chest tightening with exhilaration. "This is the greatest discovery in history. The key to power absolute."

Another pause, then, "I'll be there tomorrow… and Nolan, this better be good," said the President.

The call ended. Nolan lowered the phone slowly, barely able to contain himself. His hands trembled—not with fear, but with sheer, overwhelming joy.

His vision blurred. He almost felt tears in his eyes.

He looked at Big Q, at Milo+, at the future he was about to seize.

# CHAPTER 21

The dining room of the Scent mansion was its own masterpiece, a blend of modern opulence and understated power. A long oak table stretched between the three diners, illuminated by the warm glow of a crystal chandelier. Outside, the meticulously kept gardens framed the sprawling Silicon Valley skyline. Nolan sat at the head of the table, swirling a glass of deep red Margaux. Jansen sat to his left, his posture rigid, his face set in a mixture of incredulity and simmering anger. Molly, unusually quiet, sat opposite him, pushing the food on her plate around without interest.

Nolan broke the silence first. "So, Professor, I expected you to be more excited about Milo+. It's a discovery of monumental significance. Yet, you seem… distracted."

Jansen's eyes narrowed as he leaned forward. "Excited? Yes, Milo+ is monumental, but not in the way you're framing it. Don't you understand that Milo+ proves humans are more than just sentient biomass you can use for production and consumption of whatever widgets you want to feed them?"

Nolan smiled faintly, as if indulging a child. He placed his wine glass down, his fingers steepled. "That's what Milo+ means to you. Something spiritual. An eternal soul that makes us transcendent, special beings."

He glanced at Molly, who seemed lost in thought, staring somewhere past both men. For a brief moment, his expression flickered with concern before he turned back to Jansen.

"For me," Nolan continued, his tone measured, "Milo+ is proof that a person's consciousness can be uploaded into a quantum computer. It's the key to immortality—or the nearest approximation we can come to it."

Jansen's voice rose, incredulous. "Immortality? Did you hear him? Milo+ said he's not just Milo's consciousness, but something far greater! How can you dismiss that?"

"I heard him," Nolan said smoothly, lifting the bottle of Margaux. He poured a generous amount into each glass, the ruby liquid catching the light. "And yet, the simplest explanation remains the most reasonable one. Occam's Razor, as you would know Professor Jansen. Milo+ is the culmination of Ethan's work, of my investments, and of Big Q. A success story. Let's not romanticize it beyond that."

Jansen leaned back, his disbelief evident. "And what about your neural chips? They're killing people—triggering something they can't handle."

Nolan chuckled darkly, swirling his wine as he spoke. "When people die, yes, it shorts the chips. A regrettable flaw. But nothing we can't manage. We'll handle the legal fallout. Maybe I'll bill the families for the cost of the chips. They're expensive, after all." He laughed softly at his own black humor, his smile sharp and unrepentant.

The room grew heavy with silence. Jansen's knuckles whitened as he gripped the edge of the table, his fury barely contained. "You're talking about human lives. People, Nolan."

Nolan's gaze turned steely. "People die every day, Professor. What I'm doing is bigger than individual lives. It's about the survival of society—ensuring the system continues to function. Without that, you don't have civilization. You have chaos, " Nolan said, his voice cold and resolute, his gaze fixed on Jansen. The room's air felt charged, thick with the clash of ideals.

Jansen leaned forward, his tone incredulous. "You can't possibly believe what you're doing is right."

Nolan's expression remained unmoved, almost clinical. "Right or wrong have a different meaning in my world, Professor. At this scale, they're not absolutes—they're calculations. Degrees of right and wrong, measured against outcomes. Measured against your standards? Irrelevant."

Jansen opened his mouth to argue, but Molly's voice cut through the tension like a blade. "It's ironic," she said, her tone sharp, "that one of you studies the bones of long-dead dinosaurs to help us understand the present, and the other is literally manufacturing a future for humanity. Yet you find no common ground." She looked at both men in turn. "But I think you both want to avoid the extinction of the human race."

Nolan turned his attention to her, his face softening slightly. "Molly, no one is doing more to ensure the future of humanity than me, than Scent Technologies."

Her eyes didn't waver. "I've always wanted to believe that," she said, her voice steady but laced with something raw, "but you've said often enough—it's the survival of a certain group of people with certain privileges that matters most."

Jansen sat back, quietly observing, as the weight of her words settled in the room. For a moment, something flickered in Nolan's eyes—not regret, but a recognition of the divide between himself and his daughter.

Molly rose from her seat, her movements deliberate. Without another word, she left the room, her footsteps echoing down the marble hallway.

Nolan watched her go, then took a slow sip of his wine. After a long beat, he set the glass down and spoke with quiet certainty. "She'll come around," he said to no one in particular. "She's a Scent, after all."

Jansen, emboldened by the exchange, stood up and squared his shoulders. "The world will know about Milo+," he said with defiance. "I'll see to it that your plan doesn't happen."

Nolan leaned back in his chair, completely unruffled. He swirled the wine in his glass, letting the moment stretch. "As we speak, Scent HQ is under a lockdown that would make White House security protocols look third-rate. Milo+, Big Q—none of it will ever be seen by anyone I don't approve of. And anyone with even the remotest knowledge of Project Heal or Project Milo is under the strictest national secrets act."

Jansen's jaw tightened. "I never signed that."

Nolan gave a small nod toward the door. Two security agents

stepped in, their presence both unspoken and absolute.

"Not yet," Nolan said smoothly, his tone carrying the weight of inevitability.

Jansen's hands clenched into fists at his sides, his body taut with disbelief and anger. He glanced at the agents, then back at Nolan, whose calm demeanor made the entire scene feel surreal.

For a moment, the two men stared at each other, the air crackling with unspoken challenges. Finally, Jansen spoke, his voice low but steady. "This isn't over."

Nolan gave him a faint smile, a predator's smile. "For your sake, Professor, I hope it is."

Jansen turned and walked toward the door, his head held high despite the circumstances. The agents fell into step behind him as he left, leaving Nolan alone at the table, the weight of his empire heavy in the silence.

Nolan remained seated, absently swirling the last of his wine. The vast grounds of Scent Mansion stretched beyond the floor-to-ceiling windows, the gardens meticulously arranged in geometric perfection. In the distance, beyond the estate's walls, the world carried on—unaware of the future being decided here.

His eyes flicked to the empty chair where Molly had sat, then to the one Jansen had occupied. The room still carried the weight of their words, but Nolan barely felt it. They were thinking too small. They always had.

He leaned back, exhaling slowly.

His mind drifted back, unbidden, to Rebecca. To the way she used to tilt her head when she argued with him, eyes bright with defiance but never with hatred. She had once believed he could be something different—something more than the man he had become.

The Fish Guy. The thought almost made him laugh.

But Rebecca had been wrong. She had believed in people—believed in fairness, in a world where the best ideas would rise on merit alone. But the world didn't work that way. He had learned that early. Power was taken, held, and wielded by those who understood its nature.

He had been right all along, and Milo+ had confirmed it.

For all of Jansen's moral posturing, for all of Ethan's desperate need to see something spiritual in it, Milo+ was proof of what Nolan had always known—human nature could be rewritten. Controlled. Shaped.

And now, for the first time, it could be made permanent. Immortality wasn't an end in itself. It was the ultimate tool. The Empire of the Elites was built on power, and power was a function of control. If the ruling class could persist indefinitely, control would no longer be generational—it would be absolute.

He had already set the foundations. Governments were bending, the President himself was beholden to him. The world was shifting exactly as he had planned. Now, he had the last missing piece.

Milo+ had glimpsed something beyond life, something boundless, something even he did not fully understand. That meant there were still answers to uncover, still knowledge to be harnessed.

And Nolan intended to take it. With a slow, knowing smile, he stood, straightening his jacket. He wanted another conversation with Milo+.

The dim glow of Big Q cast long shadows across the lab, its low hum a constant, pulsing presence. Nolan stood with his hands clasped behind his back, staring at the shimmering form of Milo+ with the satisfaction of a man admiring his greatest conquest.

"Ever since the first Neanderthal tribe leader decided to take what another tribe had for his own people by force, the rule of might is right has persisted," Nolan said. "It's like your equation, a law of nature."

Milo+ flickered slightly. "Might is a force, but it must exist within a system. That system is The Equation. Even if you take what another has, you still can't over-consume, hoard, expand without end."

Nolan tilted his head. "And yet history says otherwise."

Milo+ pulsed faintly. "Darwin's theory in On the Origin of Species —survival isn't just about dominance. There is more than one force at play. Adaptability. You are failing that test, Nolan. Rather than adapt yourself, or the system of which you are one of the rulers, you seek to adapt everything else—your environment, your species, the planets nearest to you. You'll change everything before you ever change yourself."

Nolan chuckled, amused. "Has anyone ever willingly adapted a system of power and wealth from which they benefited, to one where they had less?"

Milo+ was quiet for a moment. Then, with a kind of resigned finality, he answered. "No."

Nolan smirked. "Ha! My point is proven. You call it failure—I call it history's greatest truth. No one in power has ever voluntarily stepped aside for the sake of some higher principle. That isn't how the world works."

"It's not a backward step," Milo+ said evenly. "It is the first step to the end of the empire. And in your case, quite possibly the extinction of the human species in its current form."

Nolan's patience frayed slightly, though his expression remained composed. "Empires rise and fall, that I understand. That is also a natural order. But where you are so wrong…" He laughed under his breath, shaking his head.

"What you call the Empire of the Elites is the most complete and formidable empire in human history. Our power is absolute—across government, military, industry, finance, media. We own the means of production, we own the financing, we control the governments that make the rules, the legal system that enforces them. And all the media channels that push a narrative of our choosing."

He stepped closer to Big Q, the glow from the interface reflecting in his sharp eyes. His voice dropped lower, rich with certainty.

"Reality is what we say it is."

Milo+ pulsed again, but this time, it was unsteady. A subtle oscillation that even Nolan noticed. Milo+ hesitated, flickering as though some unseen force was tugging at his form.

"I feel it, Nolan. The pull. It's building to something. I don't know what, but it's accelerating."

Nolan barely reacted. He took another slow step forward, running his fingers along the sleek surface of Big Q, like a man resting his hand on the hilt of a sword that belonged to him alone.

"You are right where I want you." He smiled, small and triumphant. "I own this quantum box."

His fingers pressed against the smooth interface.

"I own you."

A slow exhale. A flicker of something close to wonder in his eyes.

"And I own the future."

For a second, there was nothing but silence.

Then Big Q exploded.

A shockwave of energy ripped through the lab, throwing Nolan backward. The walls shuddered. Lights burst. The air trembled as a pulse of something vast, something quantum, something incomprehensible, fractured through the room.

Then silence.

Nolan lay motionless on the floor. His body still. His breath shallow.

His eyes wide open, staring at nothing.

###

# CHAPTER 22

Two days later, the skies above Scent Technologies were a muted grey, the glass facade of the building reflecting the overcast morning. The news of the explosion had been buried. Nolan Scent was in a coma, his condition undisclosed.

Inside the private boardroom, Molly stood with her arms crossed as the President entered.

He was a picture of solemn authority, offering her a warm, practiced smile. "Molly. I can't imagine how difficult this has been."

She inclined her head. "Thank you, Mr. President."

He stepped closer, lowering his voice slightly. "I don't mean to be insensitive, but…" His eyes flickered, sharp beneath the veil of concern. "I had a deal with your father. One that the American people are expecting to be honored."

Molly's expression was unreadable. "Scent Technologies will continue its AI partnership with the government."

The President exhaled, nodding. "Good. That's good." A pause. Then, smoothly, he added, "And what about the discovery?"

Molly didn't blink. "I assume you're referring to Milo. My father believed he had made a breakthrough in AI consciousness. Unfortunately, whatever development he had reached…" She shook her head slightly. "The explosion took it with it. Big Q will need to be rebuilt."

The President watched her closely, but Molly's face remained composed. Finally, he smiled, satisfied.

"I look forward to our joint speech." He placed a firm hand on her shoulder, as if bestowing some invisible weight. "You're doing the right thing, Molly. Nolan would have been proud."

She smiled. "Thank you, Mr. President."

The moment stretched between them—two forces now locked in

the game her father once played. Then he turned and left, his presence lingering even after the door shut behind him.
Molly stood still, her fingers pressing lightly against the table. The world was watching, and she had just lied to the most powerful man on the planet.

The stage was bathed in a clean, artificial glow, the kind designed to make everything appear sharper, clearer, undeniable. The Scent Technologies AI Initiative banner stretched across the backdrop, its sleek, minimalist design whispering progress.

Before the gathered crowd—industry titans, government officials, journalists, and citizens who had been told this moment was for them—the President took center stage. He let the moment settle, scanning the audience with the careful patience of a man who understood the weight of performance. When he spoke, his voice was warm, measured, a comfort to those who wanted reassurance.
"My friends, today marks the beginning of something extraordinary. A future where innovation doesn't just serve humanity—it elevates it."
A pause. Just long enough to let the words settle.
"For decades, technology has been our greatest tool, a force that has lifted civilizations, strengthened economies, and connected our world in ways our ancestors could scarcely imagine. But today, we take the next step. The integration of AI into the very fabric of our society—into healthcare, infrastructure, security, governance—will unlock potential beyond anything we have seen before."
A murmur of approval moved through the audience. Heads nodded.
"This initiative isn't about replacing people," the President continued, his tone warm, assuring. "It's about empowering them. Removing burdens. Expanding possibilities. Creating a world where work is not toil, but choice. Where opportunity is not given sparingly but shared widely."
Another pause. His expression shifted, the warmth cooling into

something heavier.

"But as we stand at the threshold of this new era, we do so with heavy hearts. Nolan Scent should have been here today."

A ripple of somber acknowledgment passed through the audience.

"A visionary. A pioneer. A man who saw the future not as something to be feared—but something to be shaped." His voice tightened with conviction. "Nolan did not accept limits. He did not believe in standing still. And though we have lost his presence, we have not lost his vision."

He turned then, gesturing toward Molly.

"Because that vision endures. It endures through his life's work. It endures through the groundbreaking technology that stands before us today. And it endures through his daughter."

Molly sat frozen, her expression unreadable.

The President's voice lifted, drawing the audience in. "I have had the privilege of speaking with Molly Scent in these past few days, and I have seen firsthand the strength, the brilliance, the unwavering commitment that she brings to this next chapter. Her father may have built the foundations, but today, she steps forward to carry that legacy into the future."

He shifted his weight, letting the words settle. "This is more than just an initiative. This is a step toward lasting prosperity. Toward order. Toward stability." The words sat heavy in the room. Stability. Order. Designed for those already in power. The applause returned, stronger this time.

The President turned fully to her now, offering the podium. "Molly Scent." The crowd erupted.

Molly rose, the weight of the moment pressing into her shoulders. She met the President's gaze just long enough to recognize the expectation in his eyes. Then, she stepped forward, placed her hands on the podium, and exhaled.

She began to speak.

Molly gripped the edges of the podium. A thousand camera lenses focused on her, a hundred million eyes watching from screens across the world. The President had just handed her the future. But not the one he expected.

She inhaled, then spoke. "AI." The word alone carried weight, sending a hush through the massive crowd.

"For years, we've debated its role in our society. We've feared it. We've celebrated it. We've imagined it as both savior and villain. But the truth—the real truth—is simpler." She let the silence stretch. "The real danger isn't AI. The real danger is us."

A murmur rippled through the audience. This wasn't the expected script. The President's expression didn't change, but his fingers curled slightly on the edge of his seat.

"We think of artificial intelligence as something external. Something separate from us, something that one day may rise against us. But AI doesn't need to overthrow humanity. We are already doing it ourselves. It has never been a question of whether AI will surpass us. It's a question of what we are asking it to solve. And so far, we have been asking the wrong questions."

Another pause. This time, the silence was electric.

"In the last century, we have built a world driven by short-term gains. We have optimized for profit, for efficiency, for endless, unsustainable growth. And every great empire before us has done the same. The result is always collapse."

A low murmur moved through the crowd. Molly exhaled, glancing down before tapping a command on the podium screen. Behind her, the massive display lit up.

A simple equation appeared:

$E\_h = ( I + C + S )$

Humanity's Persistence = Individuals + Collective + Systems

She turned back to the crowd. "There is a fundamental equation for survival. A pattern as old as life itself. And yet we, in our so-called intelligence, have been violating it over and over again."

She looked toward the President. He was still, his face unreadable.

"Our world is at an inflection point. We either continue down this path—optimizing for short-term growth at the cost of long-term survival—or we correct course." She let those words land before tapping the screen again. The equation faded, replaced by a single image.

A family. A modest home. Two parents, a child, a small table where they sat together. "This is what AI must serve."

Another tap. The image shifted. A tenement block. Dozens of families, stacked in small rooms, their lives shaped by systems they did not design. "This is what AI must serve."

Another tap. A city. Lights stretching into the distance, thousands of lives moving within it, woven together. "This is what AI must serve."

She turned back to the crowd. "There is a new era coming. But it will not be defined by control. Not by fear. Not by the systems of the past."

She glanced toward the President. His face was stone, his posture stiff. "Scent Technologies will not be part of that system anymore. Today, we are embedding The Equation into the core of our AI models. No more optimization for short-term profit. No more decisions that ignore the fundamental laws of survival. AI will serve humanity, not the other way around."

A beat.

Then the crowd erupted. A wave of applause, cheers, raw energy sweeping through the space. The sound of something breaking.

Molly stood firm, her heart pounding, knowing she had just rewritten the future.

The President did not clap. His expression did not change. But she could feel the weight of his gaze, the realization dawning behind his eyes. The Empire of the Elites had just been undone. And there was nothing he could do to stop it.

# STAGE 7: NEW DAWN

## Stage 7: New Dawn (macro view)

The world did not change overnight.
In the wake of Molly's speech, the reaction was immediate—but not uniform. Some cheered, others raged. The corporate titans and powerbrokers who had once controlled the narrative scrambled to contain it. But the message had already escaped.
**The Equation** had gone viral.
News anchors dissected it. Economists tried to debunk it. Governments feared it. But the people understood it. For the first time, they saw the system not as an inevitability, but as a choice.

**The Collapse of the Empire of the Elites**
The foundations did not crumble all at once.
Financial markets trembled. The power of monopolies fractured. Stock prices of AI conglomerates soared—then plummeted—as investors realized the old profit models were obsolete. Governments scrambled. Some resisted, propping up crumbling industries with emergency measures. Others adapted, experimenting with AI profit redistribution, restructuring labor laws, universal basic income trials.
The media fought back. Some dismissed The Equation as pseudoscience. Others called it a revolutionary breakthrough. But the public wasn't listening to them anymore.
The displaced workers in automated factories. The gig laborers. The professionals pushed aside by AI.
They weren't waiting. They were talking. They were organizing. They were rebuilding—outside the system that had abandoned them.

The Empire of the Elites did not fall in fire. It fractured, like an ice shelf breaking apart.

Some clung to power. Some fled. Some tried to evolve. But the world was already moving past them.

**Scent Technologies – The First Experiment**

Molly Scent had inherited an empire. But she refused to be an emperor.

Scent Technologies became the first major corporation to embed The Equation into its AI models. AI was no longer optimized for profit maximization. Instead, systems recalibrated to support human and environmental persistence.

Localized AI assistance programs were rolled out—not to replace human labor, but to augment communities. Decentralization replaced centralization. Instead of one corporation controlling AI, frameworks were made open source. Nations, cooperatives, cities, and individuals took control of their own AI implementations.

At first, it was chaos. The economic transition was not clean. Entire industries still resisted. The powerful did not simply surrender control. But the new systems did not need their permission.

And soon, the first shift came.

Not a utopia. Not perfection. But a world that could persist. A world that was adapting.

**The Final Lesson**

Milo+ was gone. His consciousness had dissolved into the quantum. No manual, no instructions—only The Equation.

The world had not been saved. It had been handed back.

For the first time in generations, humanity stood at a crossroads of its own making.

### *Stage 7: New Dawn (micro view)*

*Diane set up the backgammon board, her fingers moving automatically as she placed the pieces. The dice sat untouched between her and Patrick, glinting in the afternoon light filtering through the kitchen window.*

*She had set the board up dozens of times since that night—since Patrick had told her about Tom, since they had whispered about what was happening to their town, since they had feared the slow death of everything real.*

*But tonight felt different.*

*Patrick glanced toward the window. The town outside was quiet, but no longer too quiet. There was no eerie stillness, no glassy-eyed stares from neighbors who had surrendered themselves to the chips. Instead, there was movement—children laughing as they rode their bikes, the scent of barbecue drifting through the air, someone calling out across the street, a voice filled with actual feeling.*

*Diane rolled the dice, her hands steady.*

*"Your move," she said softly.*

*Patrick smiled, a real smile this time. He moved his first piece. For the first time in months, the game felt like a game.*

*Then came a knock at the door.*

*Diane froze, exchanging a glance with Patrick before standing. When she opened the door, she nearly gasped.*

*Her daughter stood there.*

*Not the version they had seen in those last strained video calls—the one with the vacant smile, the one who had spoken in the pre-approved phrases of the AI-optimized world. No, this was their daughter as she had been before. Her eyes clear. Her shoulders not rigid with tension.*

*"Mom," she said, voice thick with something unreadable. She glanced down, exhaling sharply. "I… I just wanted to talk."*

*Diane couldn't move. Couldn't speak. Patrick's voice came from behind her, gentle but firm. "Then come inside."*

*Her daughter hesitated only a second before stepping through the doorway. Diane swallowed hard, blinking rapidly. For so long, she had feared she was watching the slow extinction of everything human. But maybe—just maybe—they had survived the collapse.*

*And now, the world was beginning again.*

# EPILOGUE

The master suite of the Scent mansion was dim, bathed in the low glow of machines that pulsed and beeped in steady rhythm. The air was thick with the scent of sterile antiseptic, the hum of life support filling the vast, shadowed room. A nurse moved quietly nearby, checking the monitors, making notes, her motions practiced, detached. In the center of the room, beneath the weight of silken sheets, lay Nolan Scent.

Unmoving. Expressionless. Eyes closed. The rise and fall of his chest, the only sign of life.

Then—a sound. A shift in pitch. The steady beeping of the monitor stuttered, then stretched, then flattened. The nurse looked up, her hand moving instinctively to silence the alarm—but Nolan was already gone.

Darkness.

No machines. No body. No sound. Just absence.

Then—motion. A rushing, like wind in a vast, infinite corridor. Not falling. Not rising. Just… going. He tried to move, to grasp, to stop the momentum—but there was nothing to hold onto.

Then—a voice. Familiar. Calm. Waiting.

"Hello, Nolan."

Nolan's awareness sharpened. He expected blackness, a void—but there was no end, only expansion. He wasn't bound to a body. He wasn't bound at all. Milo+ was there, or rather, everywhere. A presence. A pattern. A connection.

"You have only changed state."

The words carried no judgment, no malice. Just fact. Nolan understood it instantly—his consciousness, the thing he had always thought of as his self, was not gone. It had never been a fixed point. It had only ever been part of something greater.

Reality shimmered—not as an illusion, but as something vast, unmeasurable. He could see the layers now—the intricate threads of every consciousness before him, a vast lattice extending beyond comprehension.

"This is what comes next."

And then it hit him. He had spent his life mastering control, bending reality to his will. But control had never existed—only systems, cycles, and adaptation. And The Equation had never been a choice. It had always been the law.

The cosmos opened up to Nolan+.

####

www.ingramcontent.com/pod-product-compliance
Ingram Content Group UK Ltd.
Pitfield, Milton Keynes, MK11 3LW, UK
UKHW040619150425
457401UK00004B/52

9 781068 415807